On the verge of telling Maurizio the whole story, Terri decided against it.

It was curious how easy she found him to talk to, as though they had entry into each other's minds. It was pleasant, but it tempted her to be incautious.

"There's something more," Maurizio said, looking at her strangely, "something that you can't decide whether or not to tell me."

"No, truly, there's nothing," Terri disclaimed.

"I think there is," he urged.

"Well—I've forgotten what I was thinking," she said hastily.

She was lying, he thought. And that was a kind of relief because it fit his original ideas about her. Except that she didn't lie like an experienced schemer, but like an awkward schoolgirl....

Dear Reader,

Welcome to Silhouette **Special Edition**...welcome to romance.

The lazy, hazy days and nights of August are perfect for romantic summer stories. These wonderful books are sure to take your mind off the heat but still warm your heart.

This month's THAT SPECIAL WOMAN! selection is by Rita Award-winner Cheryl Reavis. *One of Our Own* takes us to the hot plains of Northern Arizona for a tale of destiny and love, as a family comes together in the land of the Navajo.

And this month also features two exciting spin-offs from favorite authors. Erica Spindler returns with *Baby, Come Back*, her follow-up to *Baby Mine*, and Pamela Toth tells Daniel Sixkiller's story in *The Wedding Knot*—you first met Daniel in Pamela's last Silhouette **Special Edition** novel, *Walk Away, Joe*. And not to be missed are terrific books by Lucy Gordon, Patricia McLinn and Trisha Alexander.

I hope you enjoy this book, and the rest of the summer!

Sincerely,

Tara Gavin
Senior Editor

Please address questions and book requests to:
Silhouette Reader Service
U.S.: 3010 Walden Ave., P.O. Box 1325, Buffalo, NY 14269
Canadian: P.O. Box 609, Fort Erie, Ont. L2A 5X3

LUCY
GORDON
SEDUCED BY INNOCENCE

Published by Silhouette Books
America's Publisher of Contemporary Romance

"Only love can build a house of gold, and in every room there is a different treasure."

—Annunciata Vanzani,
mother of Maurizio Vanzani

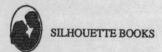 SILHOUETTE BOOKS

ISBN 0-373-09902-9

SEDUCED BY INNOCENCE

Copyright © 1994 by Lucy Gordon

Printed in U.S.A.

Books by Lucy Gordon

Silhouette Special Edition

Legacy of Fire #148
Enchantment in Venice #185
Bought Woman #547
Outcast Woman #749
Seduced by Innocence #902

Silhouette Desire

Take All Myself #164
The Judgement of Paris #179
A Coldhearted Man #245
My Only Love, My Only Hate #317
A Fragile Beauty #333
Just Good Friends #363
Eagle's Prey #380
For Love Alone #416
Vengeance Is Mine #493
Convicted of Love #544
The Sicilian #627
On His Honor #669
Married in Haste #777
Uncaged #864

Silhouette Romance

The Carrister Pride #306
Island of Dreams #353
Virtue and Vice #390
Once Upon a Time #420
A Pearl Beyond Price #503
Golden Boy #524
A Night of Passion #596
A Woman of Spirit #611
A True Marriage #639
Song of the Lorelei #754
Heaven and Earth #904
Instant Father #952

LUCY GORDON

met her husband-to-be in Venice, fell in love the first evening and got engaged two days later. After twenty-three years they're still happily married and now live in England with their three dogs. For twelve years Lucy was a writer for an English women's magazine. She interviewed many of the world's most interesting men, including Warren Beatty, Richard Chamberlain, Sir Roger Moore, Sir Alec Guinness and Sir John Gielgud.

In 1985 she won the *Romantic Times* Reviewer's Choice Award for Outstanding Series Romance Author. She also won a Golden Leaf Award from the New Jersey Chapter of the RWA, was a finalist in the RWA Golden Medallion contest in 1988 and won the 1990 Rita Award in the Best Traditional Romance category for *Song of the Lorelei*.

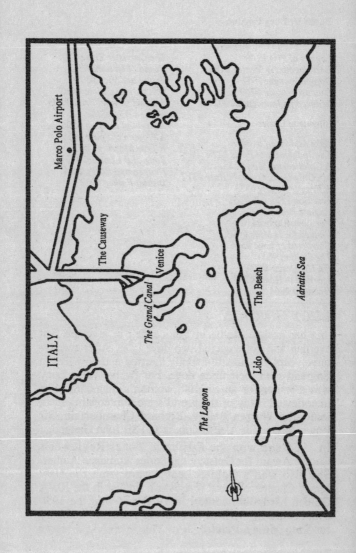

ITALY

Marco Polo Airport

The Causeway

The Grand Canal

Venice

The Lagoon

Lido

The Beach

Adriatic Sea

Chapter One

Terri Wainright's first sight of Maurizio Vanzani came so soon after her first sight of Venice that always afterward they were joined in her mind.

It began with the motorboat trip from the airport and along the Grand Canal to her hotel. At first she tried to take in details but eventually, overwhelmed by the heartbreaking beauty of the city on the water— even in the gray November weather—she sat back and drank it all in with a sense of wonder. Then the boat approached the Midas Hotel, and turned into a small side canal where a flight of steps led up from the water. And there stood a tall, raven-haired man, watching her arrival.

His eyes seemed to be fixed intently on Terri, as if he'd been standing there for a long time, waiting for her and her only. She gave herself a little shake and told herself not to be absurd. This must be the porter, and like any good hotel employee he was adept at making guests feel that only they mattered. That was the true reason for the searching look he kept on her from eyes so dark that they were almost black. Yet she still couldn't rid herself of the strange sensation that her arrival was somehow significant to him.

When the boat was secure, he reached out to help her, and her small pale hand was enveloped in his large brown one. She had a disconcerting awareness of enormous power held in check, and for a moment she was conscious of everything about him, the height of his hard, lean body, the breadth of his heavily muscled shoulders and the heat of his flesh, communicating itself to her through the firm grip of his fingers. "Welcome to the Hotel Midas," he said in a voice of such rich, bass beauty that she almost stared. "I hope you had a good flight from England."

"Excellent, thank you," she said.

"A few moments to check in, and I will show you to your room." He led her to the reception desk and stood waiting while she handed over her passport and filled in a form. Then he took her cases and led the way across a cool marble floor into an elevator.

On the journey up two floors, she had the chance to study his swarthy coloring and the air of presence and authority that surrounded him like an aura. It combined oddly with the menial task he was performing, and she wondered if he was a gambler down on his luck. The Midas was famous not only as one of the best hotels in Venice, but as a casino where fortunes were won and lost on the turn of a card. There were tales of men who'd walked in wealthy and staggered out hours later with only the clothes they wore. Perhaps he was one of them, and he simply needed a job.

"Here is your room, *signorina*," he said at last, throwing open a pair of double doors. Terri gasped at the luxury within.

"I think there must be some mistake," she said hurriedly. "This can't be the room I booked."

"You're quite right. The booking clerk made a mistake. The rooms in the price range you asked for were already taken and he double booked. The management doesn't want you to lose by this, so you've been put in a superior accommodation—at no extra charge, of course."

It sounded perfectly reasonable, yet it somehow troubled Terri. She tried to dismiss the feeling as just nerves. This whole trip, with so much depending on it, made her nervous. She was fearful of what she might find, yet she was driven on.

He set down her suitcases and went to throw open the shutters that led to a balcony, revealing a view over the Grand Canal that made Terri gasp. The better light also showed her a wine cooler, filled with ice, from which the man removed a bottle of champagne. "But I didn't order—" Terri began to protest.

"This is a normal courtesy of the management with this suite," he interrupted her smoothly, handing her a brimming glass. As she accepted it, their eyes met briefly over the rim, and again she had an unsettling feeling, as if there was something significant in his gaze. For a moment his eyes pierced her, producing a sensation of physical shock so intense that her hand shook and both his own hands closed over hers, steadying her. She could feel the barely leashed power, but it was gone almost at once as he released her and turned away to another set of double doors. "Your bathroom is through here," he said, throwing open the doors to reveal a marble room, almost overpowering in its luxury. "Now I will leave you."

Terri hunted quickly in her purse. The man raised a hand. "That is unnecessary, *signorina*."

"Oh no—I must give you—here—" She held out a forty-thousand-lire note. It was a larger amount than she'd expected to tip, but she guessed it was normal for this palatial suite. "Please, I want you to take it," she said hurriedly.

He glanced at the note with a slight twist of the lips that made her wonder if the amount was too small, after all. The feeling that he might be laughing at her made her suddenly awkward. "That will be all, thank you," she said, speaking coolly to cover her embarrassment.

He gave her a small bow and departed. Terri sipped the cold liquid and realized that it was a fine vintage, not the semiplonk that many hotels would have used for a courtesy bottle. It was the final detail added to the world-famous luxury of the Hotel Midas, a place where she couldn't really afford to stay, but where she *must* stay, because it was the starting point for her quest for her missing brother.

How she wished Leo was with her now, to raise her spirits with his charm and lightheartedness. But Leo wasn't here. He'd vanished in Venice several weeks ago. Terri would have liked to start her search in the little Hotel Busoni, where Leo had stayed, but that had closed for the winter. So she'd chosen the Midas, whose casino had drawn her volatile brother like a moth to the flame. Somehow she *must* find Leo, but she had a sense of advancing into a void.

Terri, or Teresa as she'd been born, and Leo, were twins who complemented each other: Leo, easygoing, spontaneous, fun loving, and Terri, serious, gentle, reserved. Their sharply different qualities had dovetailed, making them lifelong allies against a confusing world, where nothing was quite as it seemed.

As a child and an adolescent, Terri had never been certain who she was. Her father, Carlo Mantini, had been a short, swarthy Italian, while her mother, Madge, was English with a stocky figure, solid features and hair of an indeterminate color that she refused to dye or arrange elegantly. "I've got no patience with that sort of nonsense," she used to say firmly. "Makeup and folderols are for those with time to play." She would look at her husband as she said this, as though blaming him for something, but Carlo had become prosperous through his own restaurant, and Madge could have had luxuries and "time to play" if she'd wanted. Her husband had pressed new clothes on her, in an almost placating way, as though he were seeking forgiveness for some unspoken wrong. But Madge rarely wore them, and seemed to take a perverse, gloomy pleasure in letting herself get unattractive.

Neither of the twins were strikingly like their parents, although from some angles Leo's features had a passing resemblance to Carlo's. They were both tall, slender, fair and beautiful, and the child Terri had been puzzled when Carlo assured her she looked Italian. "But how can I be like an Italian, Papa?" she asked, studying herself critically in the mirror. "Italians are dark, like you."

"Not all of them, *piccina*," he assured her. "In the north there are many with fair hair."

"But you come from the south," she reminded him, for she loved the stories of his childhood in Naples. "So why aren't I dark?"

He didn't get the chance to answer because Madge swiftly intervened, saying it was time for the children to go to bed. That had happened often, and Terri and Leo grew to understand that Madge hated certain subjects, and would act fast to end the conversation.

Any reference to Carlo's nationality upset her, and she tried to ensure that the twins were raised as English as possible. Since they looked English, she had some success, but they loved nothing better than to hang around the restaurant, chatting to the Italian waiters. In this one matter Carlo stood up to his wife, and the children grew up speaking fluent Italian.

They adored their father, and as long as they were with him, away from Madge's antagonism, they were happy. But Carlo died when they were fourteen, and the happiness was over. The events that followed were burned into Terri's brain.

She could remember, as if it were yesterday, opening a drawer containing some of Carlo's personal possessions, seeking a memento of him that she could take and keep secretly, free from her mother's all-seeing eyes. But while she was looking through the items, Madge had stormed in. "How dare you touch your father's things without my permission?" she snapped. She'd stood there in grim fury while Terri fled the room, then she'd locked the door.

In another wife this might have looked like devotion, but there was something horrible about the way Madge raged through Carlo's possessions, as though seeking something that she must find, or die in the attempt. Then one day, Terri knew that whatever Madge was seeking, she'd found. She'd stopped searching and gone about with a dead, cold look in her eyes. She rarely spoke, but she seemed to tremble with hatred, and never more so than when she turned her eyes on her daughter.

Madge's next act shocked Leo and Terri, both for its vindictiveness and that she tried to do it in secret. By chance they discovered that she had begun moves to change their names by deed poll, wiping out Carlo's surname and calling the whole family Wainright, her own maiden name. They were too young to prevent her, but by uniting in indignant opposition, they secured a compromise. Instead of being totally eliminated, the name Mantini was relegated to the middle, with Wainright on the end. The twins disliked the arrangement and took every opportunity to emphasize their full name. Their mother countered by selling their home and moving to another part of London where nobody knew them. Gradually "Mantini" fell out of use, leaving the twins furious and appalled at the lengths to which Madge was prepared to go.

At last Terri discovered the secret of Madge's hostility with cruel, shocking suddenness. Coming home late one evening with her boyfriend, she paused outside the front door for an innocent good-night kiss, then went into the house, and straight into Madge's open hand.

"*Slut,*" Madge seethed, striking Terri again and again across the face.

Terri had vainly tried to fend her off, but Madge was releasing the rage of years. "Slut!" she repeated. "*Slut, slut, slut.*"

At last she'd stopped, and gasping, looked down at the weeping girl who'd collapsed into a chair. "Just like your mother," she said sourly.

Terri raised a streaming face. "But you're my—"

"Me? I'm not your mother. You come from an Italian slut, a whore who slept around with married men."

In ten hideous minutes Madge spewed out the bitter truth that had eaten away at her for years. Terri and Leo were adopted, not Madge's children at all. "But you're *his* kids," Madge seethed. "He never admitted it but I knew. He said one of his waitresses was in trouble, and we took her children so that she could go back to Italy and start afresh. He never admitted that *he* was the one who'd got her into trouble. To the end of his days he never admitted the truth, but I always knew."

Terri had never even suspected that she was adopted, and the sudden discovery, in an atmosphere of hate, was like a blow over the heart. But there was more to come. Now she discovered what Madge had been searching for among her husband's things.

"Look at this," Madge snapped, thrusting a newspaper cutting into the girl's face. "He kept it all these years."

The cutting came from an Italian paper and announced the marriage of Elena Fresnio to Count Francisco Calvani. There was a photograph of the bride and groom, clear enough to show that Elena was as blond as a baby.

"Look at her, standing there in a white dress and veil, looking as though butter wouldn't melt in her mouth," Madge sneered. "And all the time the little whore had a pair of bastards by a married man."

"You don't—know it was her." Terri choked on her words.

"I saw her in the restaurant when she'd just arrived," Madge shouted. "I know her face and her name. Your father had this sent to him from Italy, five years later, and he kept it all his life to remind him of the slut who bore his brats."

"Don't," Terri screamed, covering her ears. "If she was my mother, she wasn't a slut."

"That's a fine piece of reasoning," Madge said contemptuously. "But it works the other way around. She was a slut, you're a slut's daughter and you're turning out just like her."

Madge had burst into raucous sobs and run away. They'd never spoken of it again.

Leo had been staying with friends at the time, and knew nothing of the dreadful scene. When he returned, Terri told him that they were adopted, but nothing more; nothing about Elena. She couldn't bear to speak of that. And so she was left completely alone with her shock and misery, to come to terms with it as best she could.

As she grew older, Terri's natural generosity enabled her to pity Madge, miserable at her husband's infidelity, gnawed at by jealousy and the pain of having to care for his unacknowledged children. But it was harder to forgive the cruel way she herself had been made a scapegoat at a particularly vulnerable time in her life. She was fifteen, just becoming aware of her flowering beauty and sexuality, but her budding pride in herself was stopped dead. Madge's cry of "Slut" echoed in her ears, freezing her physical and emotional sensations, turning her into an iceberg. At twenty-three she was still a virgin.

Madge had died earlier that year, and at last Terri could bring herself to tell Leo about Elena. He became eager to find his natural mother. She'd urged him to be cautious, thinking that the Countess Calvani might not welcome a grown son appearing in her life after all these years, but Leo's affectionate nature made it impossible for him to believe this.

"All right, think of her husband," Terri urged. "She's probably never told him."

"I won't give away her secret," Leo promised. "I just want to see her and talk to her. Look." He took out his passport bearing the name Leo Mantini Wainright. "Remember how mad we were when Mum insisted on getting us these passports?"

"Yes, for a 'foreign holiday' that never happened," Terri remembered. "I understand why, now."

"It was just her way of getting our new names on official documents," Leo agreed. "But she did me a favor. I'll travel as Leo Wainright. The Countess Calvani doesn't know that name. There's nothing to give me away."

"Except your face," Terri said. Leo's likeness to Carlo had grown more pronounced with time.

"After all these years? Papa's hair was dark, so was his complexion. Mine are fair. It's as good as a disguise. She need never know who I am. If it seems like she doesn't want to know me, I'll just quietly creep away."

By now they each owned half in three flourishing restaurants, and combined with Terri's work as a translator and Leo's jewelry designs, this brought in enough to make them modestly prosperous. Leo blithely put his work on hold, drew out his last penny from the bank and took off for Italy. He'd gone straight to Venice where the Count and Countess Calvani owned a splendid palazzo on the Grand Canal, and waited for Elena to return from a trip to America. He occupied his time by hanging around the Calvani Art Gallery, which the family owned, and even obtained a part-time job.

"The countess runs the gallery, so when she comes back I'll get to know her this way," he explained on one of his calls home. "It's all working out beautifully."

He'd taken a room at the Busoni, a small, modestly priced place, which earned Terri's approval. But he spoiled this piece of common sense by spending many of his evenings at the casino in the Hotel Midas, which worried Terri. But in his calls home, Leo was always cheerful, making light of his losses. At last he said that Elena had finally arrived in Venice. He'd made contact with her, but cautiously at first. "As far as she knows, I'm just a casual worker," he'd promised Terri. "And I've not said anything. But I've had lunch with her."

"On your own?"

"Well—not exactly. Every week she gathers up five or six of the gallery people and takes them off to lunch. Last time, I managed to get included by hanging around and looking forlorn. I'm good at that."

"I know," Terri said, smiling at the fond memories this conjured up. "Did you get to talk to her?"

"Only a little. But next day, she had another lunch party and I was invited again. She made me sit beside her."

"I thought you said these lunches only happened once a week."

"They usually do, but she had another the next day. It's as though she wanted an excuse to talk to me again—"

"Or because she's been away and is making up for lost time with her staff," Terri said in a warning tone. "Leo, don't jump to conclusions. Did she actually make you sit next to her or did you fix it that way?"

"Well, a bit of both," he conceded reluctantly. "But she did want to talk to me, and I'm sure she guesses something."

"Leo, be careful—"

"I won't say a word, I promise. I'll wait for her to pick the moment."

He'd followed this up with an excited letter in which he said it all again in greater detail. Terri had read the letter with a frown, wondering just how much her adorable brother was deluding himself.

And then, suddenly, there was silence. No calls, no letters. When she tried to call the hotel, the line was dead. Her frantic inquiries to the Italian operator produced the suggestion that since the summer was over, the hotel had probably closed. This comforted her but only briefly. If Leo had been forced to move, why hadn't he called from his new address? She was confronted by a blank. Leo had set off full of hope in the brilliant sunshine of high summer, but now the summer was over, and he'd simply vanished from the face of the earth.

She'd determined to go in search of him, but the need to finish all her current work had delayed her departure until November. She'd checked into the Midas because it was one of her only three points of reference. The others were the Calvani Art Gallery and the Busoni hotel. Now she was here, and what seemed so simple when she was planning it, suddenly seemed like trying to penetrate a maze. She had little idea what to do next.

A knock on the door brought her out of her reverie. She opened it to find a young man standing there in the deep gold uniform of the hotel. "Your other suitcases, *signorina*."

"Goodness, I didn't realize there were any missing. I thought the other porter brought them all up."

The young man frowned. "The other porter?"

"I didn't catch his name. He was very tall and dark and he wore a white shirt with short sleeves."

"Oh that's not a porter. That's Signor Maurizio."

"Oh, is he the head steward or something?"

"No, *signorina*," the young man said with a wide smile. "Maurizio Vanzani owns the Hotel Midas." He gave a slight bow and withdrew, leaving Terri with a hand covering her mouth in horror.

She should have trusted her first instincts about the man who'd greeted her. No hired hand ever wore that air of natural authority. The memory of how she'd forced a tip on him made her feel as if she were blushing all over.

At that very moment, the phone rang. Something told her that when she answered, she would hear the beautiful bass voice that sent shivers down her spine, but anticipation couldn't subdue the reaction and she felt herself tingling. His voice was even more marvelous because it hovered on the edge of a laugh. "Please try to forgive me," Maurizio said. "I never meant to deceive you."

"I should apologize to you for insulting you with that tip," Terri ventured.

He broke into a full laugh and the sound seemed to go through her. "Believe me, I've never been so agreeably insulted in my life. *Signorina,* two people who've met as strangely as we have should get to know each other properly. Tonight you will be my guest for dinner."

The abruptness of the command took her breath away and roused her indignation. "I'm not sure that will be possible," she began to say.

"You have other plans for tonight?"

"Well no, but—"

"Then there's nothing to stop you dining with me. I'll call for you at precisely eight o'clock." He hung up, leaving her slightly cross. He took a lot for granted. It would have pleased her to call him back and tell him she wasn't at his disposal, but she resisted the temptation. She needed to talk to him about Leo. And besides—unwillingly she recalled the timbre of Maurizio's voice, the power of his presence and the intent look in his dark eyes, and an unaccustomed excitement quickened inside her. He could be a valuable source of information about Leo, she repeated firmly.

"I'm warning you, you're treading on very dangerous ground," Bruno said. He was a man in late middle age with a much-lived-in face and gentle eyes. He was Maurizio's uncle, also his bookkeeper, confidant and the only person who dared speak frankly to him. Right now, he was sitting in Maurizio's room, watching as his nephew attired himself in elegant evening clothes. The stark white of the shirt accentuated his swarthy coloring, and the gleam of his cuff links was pure gold. "Very dangerous."

"I'm having dinner with a lady," Maurizio said lightly. "What can be dangerous about that?"

"This particular lady is dangerous to you," Bruno said, "because you have designs on her."

"Not those sorts of designs."

"I'd be less worried if I thought you *were* trying to persuade her into your bed. Wanting to sleep with a woman is natural and sincere. What you're doing is twisted and frightening."

"Twisted?" Maurizio paused in tying his tie and stared at his uncle. "You think that *I* am twisted?" The level of his voice didn't change but there was a sudden chill in his eyes that in another era would have presaged a stiletto to the heart. But Bruno merely poured himself another glass of his nephew's best brandy, unperturbed.

"I think a man who sets out for revenge is always a little twisted," he said, "whether he knows it or not. If his soul isn't twisted at the beginning of his endeavor, it certainly will be by the end. God help you, my boy, if you ever achieve your revenge."

"I'll achieve it," Maurizio said quietly. "I have the right to it. How can you speak so? Have you forgotten Rufio?"

At once, both men's eyes turned to a large photograph on a nearby table. It showed a young man with a marked resemblance to Maurizio except that the boy was still clearly visible in his face, and his smile was carefree. He looked like someone who could brighten the day simply by being there. "Nobody could possibly forget your delightful brother," Bruno said sadly. "But he's dead and gone for nearly nine months."

"Dead but not gone," Maurizio said bitterly. "Not while I have breath in my body. I won't let his murderer go unpunished."

"He wasn't murdered," Bruno observed quietly. "He committed suicide."

"Yes. His life became unendurable to him because of a heartless woman who played with his feelings and threw him over when she grew bored."

"I don't think Elena Calvani is heartless," Bruno countered. "Naive and silly, but not heartless."

Maurizio's eyes narrowed. "Then tell me what you call a woman whose lover tells her that he's going to kill himself, and who does nothing—*nothing*—to stop him. I call her worse than heartless. I call her evil."

"Maurizio, you won't bring Rufio back by avenging him."

Maurizio turned on his uncle. "Don't speak of what you don't understand," he said angrily. "I loved him. He was my brother—more like a son to me. When our parents died, I had to raise him alone. It was two of us against the world. For years he was my only family."

"Until your disreputable uncle came wandering back from his travels and threw himself on your charity," Bruno said with a wry smile.

Maurizio didn't return the smile. "I'm not a charitable man," he said curtly. "You keep the books better than anyone else I've tried. That's why you're here."

"Is that why I also have free board and lodging and the key to the wine cellar?"

"Of course."

"At this point, any other man but you would be boasting of his own generosity and family feeling. But you'd deny having either, wouldn't you?"

"I admit to the family feeling," Maurizio said with a shrug. "It would disgrace me to turn my uncle away from my door—especially when he does his job so well."

Bruno sighed. "Was ever a man so blind to himself?"

"On the contrary. I see myself and my path ahead extremely clearly."

"And that path leads to revenge at the expense of an innocent young woman."

"Don't be fooled by appearances, Uncle. Teresa Mantini Wainright is no innocent. Elena Calvani's daughter *cannot* be innocent."

"Maurizio, I beg you to be careful," Bruno said earnestly. "Since Rufio died, I've seen you retreat into a cold place where there's no human pity, and all your energy is concentrated on your revenge against Elena. You see people only as an instrument for your purpose and you shut out awareness of them as human beings. You assume the worst of Teresa Wainright solely because of her mother, when actually you know nothing about her."

"Nothing about her?" Maurizio echoed incredulously. "I know everything of importance. I used to listen to Leo telling me about her. I always knew she would follow him to Venice. Last night, I didn't sleep because she was to arrive today. When I checked that her plane had landed, I was riven with nerves. I went down to the landing stage to wait for her boat. I stood and watched as she drew near and I saw the sun gild her hair exactly as I've seen it gild the hair of Elena Calvani.

"She's the daughter of my enemy, and through her I shall punish my brother's murderer. And that is all I need to know."

Chapter Two

Terri had brought her best clothes with her, dresses and accessories that she'd worn to parties in England, and that she thought of as elegant. But the Midas Hotel made them look dowdy. This was a place of money and glamour and her clothes were all too restrained. There was nothing figure hugging, nothing with an outrageously short skirt, nothing daring at all, and suddenly she felt like a little brown mouse. It briefly flitted across her mind that it was a pity Maurizio should think her dull, but she smothered the thought instantly. The instinct to withdraw from men's eyes was deeply ingrained in her by now.

At last she settled on a simple blue dress with a modest neckline that she adorned with a pearl pendant and pearl earrings. They were good pearls and would normally have been out of her price range, but

Leo had made the set for her as a birthday gift. Slipping the jewelry on, she felt closer to him now.

Maurizio had promised to call for her at precisely eight o'clock. As the time approached, she grew nervous. So much depended on this meeting. From a distance, she heard the deep, heavy sound of a bell beginning to toll the hour. One—two—three—

Exactly on the eighth stroke there was a knock on her door. Opening it, she found Maurizio there, dressed in a white dinner jacket that set off his tanned skin. His dark eyes were brilliant and he grinned in amusement when he saw her. "Good evening, *signorina*," he said. "Do you have any bags to be carried?"

"Don't make fun of me," she pleaded, also smiling, but blushing a little. "I feel awful about the mix-up."

"But why should you? The blame was mine. If you're ready, we can go straight down to where our table is waiting."

As they went downstairs, he said, "I have a private dining room where I sometimes entertain, but I thought you'd prefer to eat in the main restaurant and take a good look at the Midas. Some of the customers are extremely interesting."

Maurizio was a gambler, a man born to play poker, with a face that could confront disaster and reveal nothing. He'd assumed that blank face at Rufio's funeral, refusing to reveal his private agony to a curious world. The word had gone around Venice that he'd bid farewell to the young brother who'd been like a son to him without so much as a flicker of an eyelid or a tremor of the features. Those who had cause to fear him had become a little more afraid; the others merely wondered.

That perfect facial control prevented him from showing any surprise at the restrained appearance of Elena Calvani's daughter, but inwardly he was taken aback. The simple dress with its demure neckline stood out in the decadent opulence of the Midas, making her look like a nun in contrast.

The headwaiter greeted them at the entrance to the restaurant, gave a little bow and led them to a table by the window overlooking the Grand Canal. Maurizio handed her to her seat, touching her only briefly, but it was enough to give her the same impression of controlled power she'd had before. If anything, the sensation was more intense, like stepping too close to a caged tiger, watching him prowl patiently as he awaited his moment, knowing that the bars that checked him were fragile. The thought flashed across her mind: This man is dangerous.

Startled, she looked up at him and for a brief instant thought she saw something in his eyes that had nothing to do with the affability of the perfect host— something watchful, calculating. . . .

But it was gone so fast that she might have imagined it. Instead, there was a charming smile as he made sure she was settled comfortably, then he seated himself opposite her. "Is this your first visit to Venice?" he asked.

"Yes, it is."

"Then we won't talk for a few minutes while you watch the Grand Canal."

Entranced, Terri gazed out of the tall window at the great canal winding its way past. Darkness had fallen early, for winter was near, and along the banks gleamed a string of lights that were echoed and re-echoed by the dancing ripples of the canal. Gondolas glided on their way, the gondoliers dipping and rising smoothly, the oars sinking into water that seemed to be made of black satin, studded with gold.

"It's always breathtaking," Maurizio said in answer to her silent thought, "but never more so than the first time."

"Breathtaking," she agreed. For a moment the sheer beauty of her surroundings had driven everything else from her mind.

"What are you thinking?" Maurizio asked, watching her closely. He'd seen her frown slightly and lean forward.

"I was wondering about those little cabins that some but not all of the gondolas have," she replied.

"It's called a *feltz,*" Maurizio told her. "And it's a very insubstantial 'cabin,' just a roof with four struts clamped to the side of the gondola. The 'walls' are only curtains. You don't see many of them these days because most of the people who take gondolas are tourists who want to look around them. But at one time the *feltz* was very useful for concealing lovers."

To Terri's annoyance, she felt herself growing warm from head to toe. It was ridiculous that the mere mention of lovers from this vibrantly physical man had the power to make her self-conscious. Horrified, she wondered if she was actually blushing, and drew back, trying to seem indifferent.

She found a goblet in front of her, full of a pale, cold liquid. "I took the liberty of ordering your first drink," Maurizio said. "It's a specialty of the Hotel Midas, and only my head barman knows how it's made. He won't even tell me."

It was delicious. As she sipped, she glanced around at what she could see of the hotel. Everywhere, the theme of gold was repeated, but discreetly, and with fine taste. The fittings on the glass doors and tables were gold, as was the decoration on the exquisite crystal goblets. Maurizio caught her glance and understood it. "The hotel takes its name from the legendary King Midas, whose story I dare say you know," he said.

"He asked the gods to let everything he touched turn to gold," Terri remembered. "And they granted his wish. He was delighted until he touched his beloved daughter and she, too, turned to gold—beautiful but lifeless. He found himself living in luxury, but without love." She looked again at her surroundings. "Luxury but no love," she echoed. "Is that true?"

"Of the hotel? I imagine it's true of every place where people attach too much importance to money. Those who come to the casino have their minds fixed on gold and little else." Maurizio shrugged. "Only they can say whether the price they pay is worth it."

The waiter arrived. Terri left the ordering to Maurizio. When they were alone again, he took out the forty-thousand-lire note with which she'd tipped him earlier and pushed it toward her. "I can't accept this," he said with a smile.

Terri returned the smile—and the money. "But I won't take it back," she insisted.

He pushed it firmly in her direction again. "I received it under false pretenses."

Just as firmly she returned it. "Nonsense, you earned it. After all, you did carry my bags."

For a moment, their eyes met in a duel to see who was the more stubborn. Then they laughed together.

"Very well, I'll keep it," Maurizio conceded. He took out a gold pen, scribbled something on the note and showed it to her. He'd written:

No man should be too proud to carry bags or to be grateful for a tip. This lesson was taught to Maurizio Vanzani by Teresa Mantini Wainright, on the occasion of their first meeting.

At the end he'd added the date. Terri shrugged, a little embarrassed. "I didn't mean to teach you a lesson."

"Nevertheless, you've taught me a most valuable one. As you say, I did carry your bags. If I fall on hard times and lose the Midas, it's a skill I may need."

Again they laughed together and she was aware of a subtle charm beginning to creep over her. He was the most disturbingly attractive man she'd ever met. Just being with him seemed to make the air come alive.

"Tell me about yourself," he said as their food arrived and they began eating. "How does an Englishwoman come to bear an Italian name, and to speak my language so fluently?"

Of course, she thought, he'd seen her passport with its telltale middle name. "My father was Italian," she said casually. She'd already decided not to complicate matters by mentioning the adoption. "Although we lived in England, he raised my brother and me to think of ourselves as Italian as much as English."

"But you're called Wainright."

"That was my mother's doing after he died. She preferred to think of us as English." In these brief words, she skated over a depth of pain that still had the power to torment her.

"And how do you think of yourself?" he asked curiously.

"I don't really know," she mused. "I feel very English, I've been reared English. It's just—it's just that I've taken too long coming back to my roots."

Astonished, she wondered why she'd said such a thing. The words had come from her mouth as if of their own accord, with no thought to prompt them. It was only after she'd spoken that she discovered the thought was there. And it was true. "Too long," she repeated softly.

Maurizio was looking a little surprised, as though her words had touched a spring within him. "You were bound to come," he said. "Surely you realize that? Whatever your rearing may have been, blood speaks. And Italian blood does more than speak. It sings. Your roots will amaze you with their power to hold."

"I think Leo felt that," she said slowly. "Italy called him."

"You spoke of a brother—"

"Yes, Leo is my twin." Terri's heart began to beat faster as she came to the moment when she must decide just how much it was safe to tell. "He came to Venice, but his hotel closed for the winter and he moved out without telling me where he was going." She gave a little laugh that she tried to make sound natural. "He's such a wretch, always moving about, disappearing and reappearing suddenly. When I realized he'd taken off again, I got jealous. Why should he have all the fun of Italy? So I packed my bags and followed him here. Perhaps I'll get on to his trail. If not, I'll still have enjoyed myself."

It was a plausible story, and she finished it with a chuckle, meant to convey the impression that her search was a lighthearted matter.

"And also you will have discovered who you are," Maurizio said.

"Well—I think I know who I am. But I'll discover more about my roots."

"Isn't that the same thing? You may find you're more Italian than English, after all."

"I shouldn't think that's likely, not after the way I was raised."

"Don't be too sure. Italy is a jealous mother. Her children are hers alone, no matter who else has nursed them."

"I wonder," she said. "I really wonder."

Maurizio became absorbed in watching her face. It had an inward, untouched quality that puzzled him. She was so different from what he'd expected that for a moment he forgot his purpose and concentrated on watching the shifts of thought and feeling over her delicate features. She had an air of candor and warmth that touched his cynical heart like a spring breeze and he was almost tempted to take her farther along the path they'd started—or let her take him. He wasn't sure which. But then he remembered that spring had been over long ago. The early darkness that had fallen on the city was proof of that, and what was true of Venice was true of himself. What was done was done and he could afford no distractions.

With an effort, he forced himself back to reality. "Tell me about your brother. You said you're twins. Are you close?"

"Yes, we've always been closer to each other than to anyone else," Terri said with a reminiscent smile. "As long as I can recall, I've looked after him."

"You looked after him?" Maurizio asked in surprise. "Not he after you?"

Terri chuckled. "He's just a kid in many ways. Although we're the same age, I've always felt years older. Whenever he got into trouble, I talked him out of it."

"And if you were in trouble, didn't he come to your rescue?" Maurizio's face lit up with sudden humor. "Or were you never in trouble? Yes, that was it. I see you as one of those terribly neat little girls with every hair in place and an air of natural authority."

"What a dreadful picture," Terri said, laughing. "I was never like that. I was a tomboy, always in mischief."

"Now, I find that very hard to picture. You, a tomboy? You seem so—sedate."

"I was a tomboy when I was a child," Terri insisted. "Reckless, and always ready to stick my nose into everything, especially where it had no business being—according to my mother. But when I was about fifteen I—I changed."

"Of course, a girl grows up," Maurizio agreed, "but she doesn't usually alter completely."

"Well, I changed," Terri said quickly. She didn't want to explore this topic. Even in her own mind, she didn't like to dwell on the way winter had fallen on her, nipping her spring promise in the bud, freezing her heart and her senses. She hurried on. "When we were children, Leo rescued me from trees I shouldn't have climbed, from bullies. I rescued him from the wrath of the adults." Her face softened. "It's funny how someone can make you feel protective. He's a cheery soul, full of life and laughter, and quite sure he can take care of himself. It's just that somehow he's like a puppy who doesn't understand what a dangerous place the world is."

"And you do?" Maurizio was watching her face closely.

"Yes, I do," she said quietly. She became suddenly self-conscious. "I don't know what's making me talk like this. I've never discussed my feelings for Leo before."

"Perhaps you've never needed to," Maurizio said. He added softly, "It can take a long time for us to understand what people mean to us."

"You say that as if it meant something special," Terri said, watching him curiously.

After a moment, he said, "It does. I, too, had a brother whom I had to protect, because he was much younger than me, little more than a boy. I raised Rufio after our parents died and I felt more like his father than his brother. I, too, feared for him because he didn't know that the world was a dangerous place. I tried to teach him caution but—I failed."

"You talk about him in the past tense," Terri said slowly.

"Yes. Rufio is dead." Maurizio's tone was abrupt, shutting off further inquiry.

Anyone else would have been awed into silence, but Terri's quick sympathy had detected the pain behind the curtness, and she asked gently, "Has he been dead for long?"

"Nine months. He died in February, during Carnival. It's a time when we celebrate life, good food and wine and the joys of love." A shudder went through

Maurizio's big frame. "And in that time he died," he finished harshly.

"That must have been terrible for you."

"Yes, it was," Maurizio answered. "He was the closest family I had."

"You have no wife or children?" Terri asked the question simply and without archness, as though she was completely unaware that she was an attractive woman dining with an eligible man.

"Neither."

"Then you're completely alone. I'm sorry."

The sweetness of her voice touched his heart, and for a moment he could find nothing to say. This wasn't how he'd planned it. He'd known in advance what Elena Calvani's daughter would be like, and her looks had seemed to confirm it. She was beautiful in the same way as her mother, with an apparent fragility that was designed to put a man in a fever, and, he had no doubt, an inner core of steel to lure her victim to destruction.

But so far, he couldn't detect the steel. Instead, she dressed like a woman who didn't want to be noticed, and talked about her missing brother with a gentle wistfulness that had given him a pang of guilt for what he was concealing. And in her protective attitude toward Leo, she'd revealed herself as a kindred spirit, with an empathy that had taken her straight to the heart of Maurizio's loneliness. It was all wrong.

He realized that he'd fallen into a reverie when he saw her looking at him inquiringly. He forced himself to concentrate. "I'm hardly alone," he said, indicating his surroundings with a light laugh. "The owner of the Midas can never complain of too much solitude."

"But that wasn't what I— I'm sorry. It's none of my business."

He had a disconcerting desire to tell her that it *was* her business, that he would tell her anything she asked, in return for the relief of being able to talk about Rufio's loss to a sympathetic heart. The need filled him with alarm. Of course, this was just one of her seductive tricks, and he must be extra careful.

"Not at all," he said blandly. "It's very kind of you to be interested. Tell me some more about your brother."

"Actually, I was going to ask you about him. I know he came here a lot. Surely you must have seen him?"

"Many people come to the Midas... but yes, I recall Leo Wainright, a fair-haired young man, with a face very like yours. He was fascinated by art and wanted to be told about each of the pictures in the hotel."

"That's Leo," Terri said eagerly. "He was always interested in art but he felt he had to hide it because—"

"Because?"

"Because our mother didn't like it. Leo would have liked to be a painter, but he had to make do with learning how to design jewelry at evening class. She'd have stopped him doing that, too, if she could." Terri hesitated, on the verge of telling him the whole story, but decided against it. It was curious how easy she found Maurizio to talk to, as though they had natural entry into each other's minds. It was pleasant, but it tempted her to be incautious. For the moment, she was feeling her way gradually, picking up snippets of information about Leo, hopefully without attracting attention. "She felt that art was a lot of nonsense," she finished lamely.

"But that wasn't what you were going to say," Maurizio said, looking at her strangely. "There's something more, something that you couldn't decide whether or not to tell me."

"No, truly, there's nothing," Terri disclaimed.

"I think there is," he urged.

"Well—I've forgotten what I was thinking," she said hastily.

She was lying, he thought. And that was a kind of relief because it fit his original ideas about her. Except that she didn't lie like an experienced schemer, but like an awkward schoolgirl.

"I'm sorry if I'm disturbing you—"

Terri looked up quickly to see the man who'd spoken. He looked about sixty and although he was well dressed, his face suggested someone who'd knocked about the world and gotten roughed up in the process. But he'd learned kindness and wisdom, too, if his gentle, smiling eyes were anything to go by.

"My Uncle Bruno," Maurizio said, indicating the stranger.

"I won't stay long," Bruno said, "but I need your signature on a couple of forms."

"And of course it couldn't have waited until tomorrow," Maurizio said wryly.

"I thought I'd clear my desk out immediately," Bruno said placidly. "These impulses seize me sometimes."

"I should have guessed that one of them would seize you tonight," Maurizio responded. He spoke good-humoredly but with a touch of exasperation, and Terri had the sense of swirling undercurrents outside her comprehension.

Maurizio signaled a waiter to bring a fresh bottle of wine and another glass. "Sit down and join us, Bruno," he said.

"Well, if you insist." Bruno seated himself beside Terri and gave her all his attention while Maurizio flicked through the papers, adding his signature here and there.

"What do you think of our city?" Bruno asked Terri.

"I'm still new to it, but what little I've seen is magical," she answered at once.

"Ah, yes. Those who see Venice for the first time always think it magical."

She laughed. She felt relaxed and full of enchantment. "Are you trying to tell me that it isn't?"

"I'm saying that there's more than one kind of magic," Bruno said slowly. "Black magic as well as white. Venice isn't always a place of sunshine. You need to know about the shadows—secret corners where reality comes and goes and a million things are hidden. Darkness is dangerous but twilight is more dangerous still, for in the darkness we're all on our guard."

"And should I be on my guard?" she asked, half laughing, half intrigued by something in his tone that was more than just raillery.

"One should always be on guard in unfamiliar territory, *signorina*. Don't believe that things are as they seem. They almost never are. Isn't that so, nephew?" Abruptly, Bruno turned his attention to Maurizio.

"Why ask me?" Maurizio demanded with a shrug. "I'm not a poet."

"That's right, you're not. Not a poet, but a man with a fixed idea. That, too, is dangerous."

"I'm sure we're boring the *signorina,*" Maurizio said coolly.

Bruno drained his glass. "Now I'll leave, for I sense that I've outstayed my welcome."

"Not with me," Terri said instantly.

Bruno's answer was an enigmatic smile at Maurizio. Then he was gone.

"Did he mean anything by all that?" she asked.

"My uncle is a poet. He talks riddles and sees things that aren't there."

But although he smiled, Terri had a strange feeling that he was no longer at ease. There was a new constraint in his manner and she, too, felt as though Bruno's intervention had broken a spell. His words "secret corners where reality comes and goes and a million things are hidden" echoed curiously in her mind. It was to find what was hidden that she'd come to Venice, a city of secrets where reality came and went.

Maurizio glanced at his watch, making a sound of impatience. "Unfortunately, it's time for me to go on duty in the casino. Will you be coming to play?"

"I'd like to," Terri told him with a smile.

But she changed her mind as they approached the entrance to the casino. The women beginning to wander in were dressed in clothes that looked as if they cost as much as Terri earned in a year. Some of them glanced at her in frank amusement, and her self-consciousness deepened. Before she entered this glamorous place, she must be able to compete on equal terms. "On second thought," she said hurriedly, "I'm a little tired after my journey. I think I'll have an early night."

"Then allow me to escort you to your room," Maurizio said gallantly. At her door he stopped, took her hand and said, "I've greatly enjoyed your company, *signorina*. May I hope to enjoy it again?"

Terri drew in a sharp breath to calm the sudden beating of her heart. Until this moment, she hadn't realized how disappointed she would have been if he hadn't singled her out again. "Oh, yes," she said quickly. Then, ashamed to sound so eager, she added, "I dare say we'll bump into each other around the hotel."

"I dare say we will," he agreed, the light of amusement in his eyes. "But did you think that was all I meant?"

Again his eyes held the look that had disturbed her before, as though everything that was happening had another meaning, a different kind of reality. It all seemed connected to the warmth that was stealing through her from her hand where he was still holding it. There was excitement in his touch and his gaze and suddenly she couldn't breathe.

"Whatever you meant," she said slowly, "you must tell me another time. Good night."

Chapter Three

Terri breakfasted in the restaurant next morning, choosing a window seat where she could see the Grand Canal in daylight. At this hour, the traffic was different to that of the evening. Now barges chugged by, laden with supplies for the hotels and restaurants. From her corner position she watched several turn in to the side entrance of the Midas where hotel workers pounced and unloaded them in minutes.

A waiter noticed her interest. "The kitchen is stocking up for the party tonight, *signorina*," he told her.

"A party?"

"Signor Maurizio has enlarged the casino and the new rooms are to be opened tonight with a big party."

"But I thought that business was falling off because it's winter—"

The waiter smiled. "That's true for other hotels, *signorina*. Business *never* falls off at the Midas." He poured her coffee and departed.

Terri pulled a map of Venice from her purse and studied it to find the Hotel Busoni, where Leo had stayed until it closed for the winter. She located it, finished her breakfast and left the Midas, confident that she could walk to the Busoni. But after a while, she realized just how different Venice was to all other cities. It wasn't merely that so many of the "streets" were water; the ones that weren't water were often no more than tiny alleys, paved with flagstones. These were called *calles,* and some of them were so narrow that by standing in the middle and stretching out her arms, she could touch both sides at once.

Without warning, a *calle* would turn into a bridge taking her over a tiny canal, called a *rio,* and into a confusing maze. Within a few minutes, she was thoroughly lost and it took her two hours to cover a mile. But at last she came to the Calle Largo, where the Busoni was situated. The little alley was narrow and mysterious and contained several tiny hotels, all of which seemed to be closed.

A chill breeze blew and Terri shivered slightly. Leo had stayed here. He'd trodden these flagstones and walked in and out of that door that was now so firmly shut. But there was no sign of him and the quiet seemed to mock her.

There were a couple of shops nearby and she was about to enter one in the hope of picking up a scrap of information when a woman appeared on the bridge at the end of the *calle* and began to walk toward her. She was middle-aged and soberly dressed with neat gray hair and a dour, purposeful air. As Terri watched her, she stopped outside the Busoni and unlocked the door. Hardly able to believe her luck, Terri stepped quickly forward and spoke to her. "Please, can I talk to you?"

"The hotel is closed for the winter, *signorina*," the woman said firmly.

"I know that. I want to ask about someone who stayed here recently."

The woman looked her up and down. "You'd better come in."

Inside, everything was shrouded in covers. Their footsteps made a hollow sound on the terrazzo floor as they headed toward the kitchen. The woman gathered up some mail and thrust it into her bag. "I come back sometimes for the mail and to see that all is well," she explained. "I am Signora Busoni and I own this hotel."

"Then you knew my brother, Leo Wainright," Terri said eagerly.

Signora Busoni gave a wry smile. "Oh, the young Englishman. I remember him—very charming but usually paid late. He kept losing his money at the Midas."

"That's Leo," Terri said at once. "Can you tell me where he went?"

The *signora* shrugged and began to make coffee. "I wasn't here on the day he left. I was spending a few days in Verona looking after my mother who was ill. My son Tonio was in charge and unfortunately he's an idiot. I came back to find everything in chaos, the books not kept properly, receipts lost, bills not paid— total disaster!"

"But did he know where Leo had gone?" Terri pressed her, trying to curb her impatience.

"Well, after I'd boxed his ears, he was a bit confused," Signora Busoni said, pushing the coffee toward Terri. "But he said Leo had gone to visit friends for the weekend."

"What friends?"

"Do you think the fool could tell me that? When I realized Leo wasn't coming back at all, I boxed Tonio's ears a few more times but it didn't make him talk any more sense."

"Not coming back at all? You mean he went to stay with friends and just vanished?"

"That's right. I cursed him when I realized he'd left owing me money, but it was all right in the end. He sent what he owed."

"Then you must know his address?" Terri said eagerly.

"No, a man came to pay his bill and collect his things."

"What was the man's name?"

The *signora* shrugged. "Rienzo—Rafaello—something like that."

"You just let him take Leo's possessions without even knowing his name?" Terri cried.

"I was very busy packing everything up to close the hotel. Besides, he must have been a friend of your brother's, or why should he pay his bill?"

"Can't you remember anything about him?" Terri asked in despair.

"Well—he wasn't a Venetian. From his accent I'd say he came from the south. And he had a large gap between his front teeth."

Terri tried one last time. "Could I talk to Tonio, please?"

"You could if I knew where he was. As soon as the doors were closed, that work-shy good-for-nothing took off. Said he was going to India, to hitchhike."

Terri could have wept. She was no nearer to finding Leo than before, and his disappearance seemed even more mysterious. "Can I have a look at his room?" she asked.

Signora Busoni sighed but didn't refuse her, and a few minutes later Terri was standing in the room Leo had occupied. The bed had been stripped bare and covers shrouded the furniture. She went through the wardrobe and the bedside drawers hoping to find a scrap of paper, or *something* that would give her a clue. But there was nothing to suggest he'd ever been there. She stood in the echoing silence and could find no sense of Leo.

She thanked Signora Busoni and went despondently out into the street. A café stood next door and she went in and ordered coffee. But when it was on the table in front of her, she simply sat staring into thin air, trying to grapple with her despair. Leo had gone away one weekend and simply vanished into thin air, and now she had no idea what to do next.

"Your coffee will get cold," came a voice from above her.

Startled, she looked straight up into the dark eyes of Maurizio. Before she could speak, he'd signaled for a fresh coffee to be set before her. "Thank you," she said. "I guess I lost track of time."

"Have you been to the Busoni to get news of your brother?"

"Yes. I thought I'd got lucky because the owner returned, but she didn't know anything. Leo went away one weekend and never came back. Someone paid his bill and took his things.''

"So he must be all right.''

"But why didn't he contact me?''

"From your description of him,'' Maurizio said thoughtfully, "he doesn't sound like the most responsible person in the world.''

"That's true,'' she said wryly. "He might simply have forgotten—or maybe he wrote and the letter went astray.''

"Will you let me give you some advice? Don't worry about Leo. I don't think he came to any harm.''

She made a valiant effort to seem nonchalant. "Oh, I'm not worried. Like I said last night, Leo is such a jumping bean that—'' She saw Maurizio looking at her and her pose collapsed. "Leo's thoughtless but he's kind. He'd have called me before this unless—*no,* I'm not going to start thinking like that. There's still the art gallery where he did some casual work. There's also the casino, where, according to Signora Busoni, he used to gamble the rent away. A waiter told me you're having a big function there tonight.''

"That's right, to celebrate the new rooms. So it will be the ideal time for you to come. All Venice will be here, not the tourists but the Venetians.''

Perhaps the Calvanis, she thought with rising excitement. Then she remembered her dull wardrobe. "I haven't anything suitable to wear,'' she mused out loud. "I saw people coming in last night and they were dressed to the nines.''

"So you must do the same,'' Maurizio said with a shrug. "If you haven't a suitable gown, it's simple to obtain one. Some of the Venetian shops sell the highest fashion.''

"I don't need the highest fashion. I don't want to look conspicuous."

Maurizio laughed, and the sound went through her like warm tremors. "Whoever heard of coming to the Midas Casino and being inconspicuous?" he declared. "When the gorgeous peacocks of Venice parade under the chandeliers, they know how the lights make them glitter, and they strive to outdo one another. Being inconspicuous isn't allowed."

"I don't really see myself as a peacock. Nature didn't make me that way."

"How do you know?" he asked at once. "There isn't one woman in a thousand who really understands how nature meant her to be. Only the beholder knows that."

His eyes were fixed intently on her, and she had a terrible temptation to ask him how he saw her. But in the same moment, she felt herself instinctively withdrawing, as she always did at the first sign of a man's interest. Part of her felt a frisson of intense pleasure at his gaze and the significance behind it, but another part, that was beyond her control, flinched.

"I know myself," she said, fighting a sudden breathlessness. "I'm no peacock. More like a little brown mouse."

Unnervingly, he leaned closer and brushed back a stray tendril of blond hair. "No little brown mouse ever had hair this shade of pale gold," he said softly. "It's the color of glamour."

"Glamour," she echoed with an awkward little laugh. "Me?"

Maurizio curled the tendril softly around his finger. "Didn't you ever read fairy tales as a child?" he asked. "The princess was usually blond, whether she was called Cinderella or Sleeping Beauty, she was as fair as a spring day, and the prince found her irresistible.''

She looked up at him, puzzled at his tone, and suddenly Maurizio felt something constrict his throat. Did ever a temptress gaze at a man from eyes so innocent and candid, so dangerously concealing of her true nature? Elena Calvani's daughter, with Elena Calvani's treacherous ways! It was all there in the lovely blue eyes, curving mouth and small, determined chin. A seductress masquerading as an ice maiden. And such a mask! So convincing that a man might almost believe it was the real thing, if he didn't know that it couldn't be.

He was assailed by a mad desire to get her out of the demure clothes she was wearing and into something that would reveal the truth about her inner nature. Then perhaps he would know peace instead of being tormented by the two conflicting sides of her. The need was like a storm within him, but no trace of it appeared on his smooth, gambler's face. "You must let me take you to a place where you can choose something suitable to wear," he told her.

"Well—perhaps some other time," Terri prevaricated. She was feeling rather overwhelmed by his energy.

"What better time than now? Come. I know the very boutique that will suit you." He took her hand and strode out of the café.

There was no question of refusing, and suddenly she didn't want to. An urgent physical excitement had blended into a feeling of happiness that swept her without warning.

After hurrying along for ten minutes, they plunged into a tiny shop, so tucked away that Terri would never have noticed it. As Maurizio swept her in, she just had time to notice a single dress in the window. It looked simple but expensive, and the fact that there was no price on it suggested it was *very* expensive. Anyone who had to ask the price couldn't afford it. "Maurizio," she tried to protest.

But he was already inside, summoning the manageress and greeting her with a kiss on the cheek. She evidently recognized him and regarded Terri with interest and curiosity. "My friend Teresa Wainright is buying new clothes," Maurizio declared. "First she needs something for the big party at the casino tonight. It must be extra special."

Signora Zena, the manageress, was tall, middle-aged and imposing. She cast appraising eyes over Terri before going to a curtained door and rattling out a series of commands. Within a few minutes, two young woman scurried in with their arms filled with gowns. "This one first," Zena declared, indicating a creation in blue.

Terri tried it on in the changing room and emerged hesitantly. The skirt was shorter than she was used to wearing, yet she was rather taken with her new, more glamorous self. But Maurizio shook his head when he saw her. "It's perfect for her," Zena declared. "Youthful and daring."

"Too daring," Maurizio insisted.

"So? The young can afford to take risks. Signorina Wainright has a perfect figure. She should show it off. Later will be too late."

"Hey, don't I get a say in this argument?" Terri asked, amused and bewildered. "I like it."

"It doesn't suit you," Maurizio said firmly. "Try something else." He saw her looking at him askance and broke into a smile that seemed to make her heart somersault. "I'm being intolerably overbearing, aren't I?"

"Yes," the two women said with one voice.

He assumed an expression of penitence that didn't fool Terri. This man was a natural autocrat and any appearance of regret was merely a device for getting his own way. Already she could divine that much about him. But it didn't matter. The fact that he cared so much what she wore caused a sweet singing inside her. He should have been back at the Midas completing his preparations for tonight, but on such a busy day he'd chosen to be here with her, trying to make her appearance fit his inner vision of her. Just to know that she figured in his inner vision gave her a feeling of excitement that was filled with delightful danger. If she was to look the way he wanted, what would he do then?

At Maurizio's insistence, she tried another dress but that didn't please him, either. He seemed unable to explain what he wanted, yet he knew exactly what he didn't want. At last Zena produced a white dress that Terri had briefly considered and discarded, and said wearily, "There's only this one left."

"I don't really want a floor-length gown," Terri began to say, and stopped when she saw Maurizio's face. "What is it?" she asked anxiously.

He seemed to come out of a dream. "Try that one on," he said with an effort.

"But it's white. I don't normally wear white. I think it looks pallid with my coloring."

"Try it," he repeated.

The dress was skintight and hugged her so closely that she had to strip off every stitch of underclothing to get a smooth line. Yet the neckline was demurely high, coming right up to her throat. There were no sleeves and the gown was cut away over the shoulders so that everything hung from the neck. Terri drew in her breath at the vision that faced her in the mirror. This was a dress for a woman who was supremely confident in her own body, yet who kept that body for herself, revealing only a little, and that in the most tantalizing and subtle manner; it was for a woman who held back, seeming to offer much yet offering nothing that couldn't be withdrawn; suggesting much, yet nothing that couldn't be denied. Only a subtle temptress could wear such a dress, and Terri simply didn't feel up to it.

"It's beautiful," she breathed, "but not for me."

"I disagree," Maurizio said in a strange voice. "I think it suits you to perfection."

"Perhaps you'd like to take a look at yourself next door," Zena suggested smoothly. "You can watch yourself walking in the mirrors." After showing Terri into a long room, one whole wall of which was taken up by mirrors, she discreetly faded away.

Terri stood for a moment, trying not to hear Madge's voice crying "Slut!" in her mind. Only a slut would wear such a dress, so calculated to warn men off and lure them on at the same time. Slowly, Terri began to walk the length of the room, watching her own movements in the mirrors. Mysteriously, her body seemed to have changed shape in some indefinable way. Now it glided as though it had been born to wear such a provocative garment. It knew just how to walk to reveal the curve of hip beneath the chaste white silk.

Maurizio's face came into her mind, his eyes warm and penetrating as she'd seen them last night. She knew he wanted her to choose this dress and the thought sent heat scurrying through her body, making her breathless. Never before had she known this unnerving sensation of having her will destroyed. She was a strong-minded woman, but all she wanted now was to look as *he* desired, and be what *he* wanted.

Slut! Slut!

"No," she breathed. "I won't listen to you. It doesn't make me a slut to feel this way. It makes me— his. But I've only known him a day. How can I be such a fool?"

She walked the length of the mirrored wall again, torn by indecision.

Maurizio, waiting outside with apparent calm, allowed Zena to press coffee on him, drinking it without tasting it. His thoughts were in that room, with Terri. Mentally he walked the floor with her, watching every sinuous movement of the dress against her hips and thighs, contrasting them with the nunlike face above. To torment a man by cloaking herself in feigned ingenuousness—Elena's daughter would have been born knowing how to do that. What was she waiting for now? Some sign that she could lead him on, perhaps? If so, she would be disappointed.

But as the minutes ticked away and she didn't appear, his nerves tautened to breaking point. "Perhaps you should go and have another word with her," he said to the manageress.

She shrugged. "Oh, no. That's the way to lose a sale. When a woman is undecided, the more time alone she has, the better."

"In that case, I'll have some more coffee." He set his cup down with a slight clatter.

Terri came to a reluctant decision. She felt like a coward because her nerve had failed her, but Madge's influence had proved too strong. She pushed her hair up high on her head in the manner the dress demanded and took one last longing look at what she might have been.

"Yes."

She opened her eyes wide at the soft violence of that word. Maurizio had entered silently and stood looking at her in the mirror. "Yes," he repeated. "Like that."

She turned, letting her soft blond hair fall. "I can't," she protested. "It's not me. I only wish it were."

In a moment he was beside her, turning her to face the mirror again. "That's because it *is* you and in your heart you know it," he insisted. His strong, brown hands swept her hair back up, leaving her neck bare, and suddenly she was overwhelmingly conscious of how close his lips were to that bare skin. "Look," he said, meeting her eyes in the mirror. "Look and see the truth of yourself." He caught up a tendril from her neck and she shivered as his fingertips brushed her. "Why do you deny it?" he whispered.

She sighed, overpoweringly tempted. "If only..."

"If onlys are for little girls. A woman takes what she wants. You want this gown because it tells you the truth about yourself, and also because *I* want you to wear it."

Overwhelmed though she was, one calm, ironic corner of Terri's mind resented this assumption and enabled her to say with a touch of annoyance, "Do I really want only what you want, Maurizio? Aren't you taking a lot for granted?"

"A lot, yes. Too much? Only you can answer that. Blame yourself for what you're doing to me." The words poured out of him in something like desperation. He was closer to losing control than he'd ever been in his life. She'd shown him the vision before threatening to snatch it away, and now he was on the rack.

And he'd blundered. He knew that was so when he saw the sudden aloofness in her eyes. She was watching him and calculating, and he'd revealed too much. He strove to get command of himself, to remember that she was a part of his plan, but it was no good. The warm, sweet scent of her filled his nostrils, making his senses riot. Her pale skin was silk under his fingers, while the dress suggested and concealed everything he wanted to know. Unable to stop himself, he drew her back against him and dropped his head so that his lips rested on her long neck. He felt the tremor that went through her, then the slight stiffening as if she were rejecting what was happening. For a moment, he almost thought she would break away from him, and the thought almost drove him to madness. He wanted her, not Elena Calvani's daughter but *her*, Teresa Wainright with her soft skin, candid eyes and air of innocent abstraction. He wanted her and he would have her.

He tightened his hold, turning her in his arms so that he could look into her face. Her head was thrown back and her lips were slightly parted, but what struck him most was the startled look in her eyes, as though she couldn't understand what was happening to her.

"Teresa . . ." The word was torn from him. *"Teresa . . ."*

He was kissing her before she knew what he was going to do, kissing her with a mad lack of restraint that made a mockery of his careful plans. There was no calculation now, only a burning desire to possess this woman, to discover the heart of her mystery and understand it, so that it ceased tormenting him. She was sweet and melting in his arms, yet with a hint of fire far back, fire that he knew would draw him on so that it could engulf and consume him.

He'd known that her pale blond beauty, so seemingly English, was but a mask for her hot Italian blood. Now he rediscovered it with new force. That mask hid the truth of her, and the truth was what he was determined to have. He forgot that he, too, hid behind a mask of steel that he kept between himself and the world. The touch of her lips on his left him feeling defenseless, open to her and all the new experiences she promised. He kissed her more deeply, reveling in the discovery of a woman unlike all others.

In the first shattering moments of his embrace, Terri tensed. The old instinctive withdrawal was still there, but it couldn't survive under the onslaught of Maurizio's passion. She'd been kissed before, but only by boys who'd politely retreated when they sensed her coolness. This was a man who would retreat before nothing, whose desire was fierce enough to melt her icy barriers. She put her arms about him, returning his kiss in a way she hadn't realized she could. But she did know it because the knowledge was born into every woman for the man who could bring it to life.

She was dizzy as his lips moved slowly over hers. The world seemed to shift underfoot so that she might

have fallen but for his arms supporting her. She closed
her eyes, wanting not to see him but simply to be totally aware of the magical new sensations that were
coursing through her. It was like being reborn, but
born with nerves that vibrated to his touch, giving
every sensation a thrilling intensity. She let her head
fall back against his shoulder, offering herself up
completely to what was happening, astounded at her
own reaction but glad of it with every fiber of her being.

Maurizio heard her sigh and drew back to look at
her. "What is it?" he murmured.

"Nothing, just—kiss me again...."

No power on earth could have made him resist that
invitation. Before her words were fully out, he covered her mouth, driving his tongue inside to seek her
more deeply.

She was aware of him not merely through her lips
but all over her body, as though the dress had melted,
leaving her naked. Once, that thought would have
embarrassed her, but now she knew that nakedness
was the right, the inevitable thing with this man. This
kiss was but the first step on the road to physical
union, and already that was what she wanted.

His tongue inside her mouth thrilled her. It was
teasing her subtly yet purposefully, evoking sensations no man had aroused in her before. In a few seconds those sensations had spread to possess her entire
body. She was hot and cold together, calm like someone who'd come home at last, yet trembling with eager discovery.

She could feel his hands roving over her body, trying to find their way to her but defeated by the dress.
She wondered wildly if he could tell that she was na-

ked underneath. If only she could be completely naked ... with him....

Maurizio was in a state of utter confusion. Desire
warred with alarm as he felt her through the thin material. Beneath this demure dress, she was wearing
nothing—the perfect temptress.

Just like her scheming mother.

The words shouted in his head, turning his blood to
ice and his desire to rage. Suddenly, Elena was there
with them, mocking him with the perfect beauty that
Rufio had found so irresistible. Rufio was dead and in
his arms he held the daughter of Rufio's murderer. A
shudder went through him and he had to fight to stop
himself from thrusting her violently away.

"What's the matter?" Terri asked, sensing his inner withdrawal.

"Nothing—that is, someone might come in. This
isn't the place—" He drew a ragged breath. "Perhaps that dress isn't right for you, after all."

"Oh, I think it is," she said, smiling eagerly. "I'm
going to buy it whatever it costs."

"But I don't think—" He stopped. He was on the
rack. Terri's eyes, full of innocent puzzlement, gazed
at him. "You must make your own choice," he said
abruptly, and strode out.

Chapter Four

In the luxurious bedroom of the Contessa Elena Calvani, the dressing-table mirror reflected a goddess. The light turned her pale blond hair into an aureole about her face, and everything about that beautiful face was perfect, cool, smooth, time defying and oddly lifeless.

She rose as Anna, her maid, took down the dress she'd chosen for this evening, a black-and-silver, figure-hugging garment that few women of forty-two would have dared to wear. But the countess's figure had been preserved by a stringent regimen of diet and massage. The same regimen had kept her jawline firm, postponing a face-lift until the last moment. When the day of reckoning had come, the operation was performed in a discreet Swiss clinic in a room on the eighteenth floor where no curious intruders could penetrate. Not until the last bruise had faded did Elena face the world again, and tonight would be her first appearance in public since her return.

Anna, the only person admitted into the secret and who'd been with her in Switzerland, helped her mistress into the dress. "The *contessa* is a work of art," she pronounced happily. "I promise you, no one will guess."

"There are plenty who will speculate," Elena said wryly.

Anna shrugged. "Of course. Perfection always inspires malice."

"Perfection." Elena echoed the word as she smoothed the dress down her thighs and considered her long, black, silken legs. "Well, perhaps—for the moment. But for how long? Nothing lasts forever, least of all perfection. And then—" A faint shudder went through her. But she recovered herself and said, "I'll wear the diamond earrings tonight."

As Anna was completing her work, the door opened and Count Francisco Calvani entered. He waited in silence until the maid had scuttled from the room in a way that bespoke dislike and fear. He was a tall lean man, with a haughty, aristocratic face that would have been handsome but for its coldness, and he regarded his wife with a look that was part complacent possession, part sneer.

"Splendid, my dear," he said when they were alone. "No woman there will be able to hold a candle to you—which, of course, is no more than I expect."

"I'm glad you feel I'll do you credit," Elena responded lightly. "I try my best."

"And your best is superb," Francisco said without relaxing the cold lines of his face. "No other woman your age would dare to wear that dress. Of course, a

figure that hasn't been ruined by child bearing—'' He
left the implication hanging in the air, but his sharp
eyes didn't miss the shadow that crossed his wife's
beautiful face.

After a moment, when she didn't reply, he continued. "I must confess I'm a little surprised that you've
chosen the Midas for your reappearance in public."

"Why should you be surprised? Everybody will be
there tonight. And Maurizio was so very insistent."

"To be sure. It's just that I thought you disliked
him."

"I have no feeling about Maurizio one way or the
other," Elena said with a shrug.

She never discussed her feelings with her husband.
Nor was she analytical, or she might have wondered
why she'd felt compelled to accept the invitation of a
man whose very name gave her a frisson of alarm. She
only knew that she had to go there, as though by
flaunting her restored beauty to the world she could
reaffirm her own courage.

She checked her face one last time. The mirror
showed her what she wanted to see, a perfect mask,
revealing nothing, not even fear, so much harder to
disguise than any other emotion.

"I'm ready," she said, picking up her black-and-
silver purse, and sauntering ahead of him out of the
room.

At the last moment, Terri had an attack of doubts.
Hanging up, flat and lifeless, the dress was plainly
outrageous and she began hunting frantically among
her other things until she found something else. Glad
to have the matter settled, she plunged into a shower,
but as the water laved over her nakedness, her flesh

began to remember Maurizio, how it had felt to be held by him, pressed close to his lean, hard body. She tried to ignore her memories but they made her blood sing, and when she stepped out of the shower, she went straight to the white dress.

She wondered if Maurizio could have been right. Perhaps there really was another side to her, a side that she herself had never suspected—or rather that had been buried beneath the weight of Madge's disapproval. Without the burden of Madge's influence, what might she have been?

Her reverie was interrupted by a knock on the door. She wondered if Maurizio had come to fetch her, but it was a bellboy with an envelope. Inside she found her ticket for the party and a voucher for two hundred pounds' worth of free chips. There was also a note from Maurizio.

> Unfortunately, my duties make it impossible for me to escort you tonight, but I hope to spend some time with you.

She smiled and put everything in her purse.

At the door to the roulette room, she presented her ticket and was directed to the place where she could exchange her voucher for chips. She was a little self-conscious about her solitary state, especially when she began to be aware of admiring glances. But she put her head up and soon had enough confidence to start looking around her at the rococo splendor of the huge room.

Heavy marble columns reared up to the ceiling, which was covered in paintings in the eighteenth-century style. Shepherds and shepherdesses postured before one another, satyrs danced through the greenery, silken lords and ladies preened and flirted. The walls were covered in huge mirrors of old venetian glass.

Maurizio quickly made his way over to her. While he was still a few feet away, she sought his eyes and found there what she wanted to see. His gaze was fixed on her, dark, intense. And suddenly she knew that he'd been watching the door. His words confirmed it.

"You came," he said softly.

"Did you think I wouldn't?"

"Until the last moment, I wasn't sure. I'm glad you're here. I wish I could be with you this evening...."

"I know you have many guests to look after."

"Unfortunately, yes. But there'll be other evenings." He gestured to a waiter who proferred champagne.

"To your success," she said, smiling and raising her glass to him. "May you have everything you dream of, and may even your most secret wishes come true."

A strange look crossed his face. "Why did you say that?" he asked quickly.

"Wished you success? But of course—"

"No—after that. About my secret wishes."

She shrugged. "Everyone has secrets. And you especially."

"Why me especially?" he asked, trying to keep the strain out of his voice. For some reason, this conversation was unnerving him.

"Because you're so—what's the word?" She saw him looking at her searchingly, and laughed. "If you could only see your face!"

"What do you read in my face, Teresa?"

"You're taking this so terribly seriously. Forget I said anything."

"No." He touched her arm, trying to subdue the shock of pleasure that pierced him at the silky beauty of her. "I don't want to forget. What is the word that you're looking for? Why must *I* especially have secrets?" He knew he was revealing too much about his thoughts, if she was shrewd enough to read them. But her expression retained its innocent clarity.

"Because you're so Venetian. Already I know that this is a city of secrets, and you're its son."

"Is that all you meant, Teresa?"

"But of course. What else could I have meant?"

He relaxed. "Do you have your chips?" he asked, trying to speak more normally.

"Yes, but there was no need—"

"Every guest tonight has the same, so don't feel embarrassed. Let me show you how to play roulette."

He led her to a table and showed her how to place her money on a number. She chose Red and laid a chip on the square. "That's not enough," Maurizio told her, scandalized. "Come, be brave. You must risk everything at once."

"I couldn't do that," she said, laughing. "I prefer to go cautiously, just at first."

Maurizio groaned. "Oh, the cautious English. You should learn to gamble properly." Before she could stop him, he'd seized all her chips and laid them on the square. The next moment, the wheel spun. Terri kept her eyes on it as it slowed and slowed . . . and stopped.

The ball was in Black 21.

"You see what comes of putting all your eggs in one basket?" Terri asked comically.

Maurizio leaned over the table and seized her chips, returning them to her. "Since I lost them for you it's only right that I should give them back," he declared. "Now, what are you going to do?"

"I'm going to make it last," she told him firmly.

"How different from your brother. Once or twice I had to restrain him in his conviction that he was beloved of the gods and couldn't possibly lose."

"That sounds exactly like Leo."

"Let's take a breath of fresh air before the place fills up," Maurizio suggested.

"It looks pretty full already," Terri said, glancing around at the buzzing room.

"This is nothing. Wait until the party really gets started," he said, guiding her to the terrace.

It was cool and pleasant outside and Terri breathed in the night air with relief. The roulette room was just above water level and from the terrace Terri had a good view of the Grand Canal with the multicolored lights strung along the bank. She could almost have touched the boats that went by. Even at this time of night the canal was busy, with gondolas splashing softly, and the sounds of faintly chugging motorboats. "Nearly midnight," Maurizio observed. "Now the casino will start to come to life."

As he spoke, a long white motorboat appeared around the curve of the canal and slowed as it neared the Midas. It was a sleek, luxurious vessel whose lines spoke of elegance and money. At it grew nearer, the lights from the hotel illuminated a man and a woman sitting in the back. The man had a bored, handsome face, and was discreetly dressed in evening attire. The woman looked frail and slight, and might have been no more than a girl.

"The Calvanis," Maurizio declared. "Good. He always loses a fortune. Luckily he can afford to."

"Luckily?" Terri echoed. "So you do care about your customers?"

Maurizio grinned. "Not at all. I'm not a soft-hearted man, Teresa. I meant luckily for me,"

Terri didn't answer. Her gaze was fixed on the woman, whose fair hair was made brilliant in the gold light from the hotel entrance. From this angle, she could see little except that Elena Calvani was daintily built and gorgeously dressed, but her heart had begun to hammer as she realized she was seeing her mother for the first time.

Or was this her mother? Had the whole thing been a mad fantasy? A mixture of excitement and fear made her grip the railing of the stone balcony tightly. She didn't notice that Maurizio was watching her closely, his face set, his eyes appraising.

At last he spoke. "The Contessa Calvani is one of the glories of Venice."

"She's certainly very beautiful," Terri said, not taking her eyes from Elena.

"Beautiful, artistic, the perfect mistress of a palazzo, and famed for her works of charity," Maurizio said. "It's such a tragedy."

"What's a tragedy?" Terri asked at once.

"That the Calvanis have no children."

"The *contessa* has—no children?" Terri echoed slowly.

If he noticed this slight change of emphasis, Maurizio's smooth face gave nothing away. "I believe it troubles her greatly," he said. "When Francisco dies, the title will go to a cousin whom he detests. I believe he'd do anything to prevent that."

"But what *can* he do?"

Maurizio shrugged and led her back into the roulette room. "Rid himself of her," he said. "A discreet divorce, or even an annulment."

"He can annul their marriage simply because she didn't give him an heir?" Terri demanded, outraged.

"That depends on why she didn't. A count expects to marry a woman with a title. But Elena was a nobody from nowhere, and he married her in defiance of his family and friends. Who knows the secrets of her past?" Maurizio shrugged. "Perhaps there's something that would explain why she's barren. He, at least, would be glad to know. There's less scandal in annulment than in divorce."

"Poor woman," Terri murmured. "She must live her life on hot coals."

"I wouldn't waste too much sympathy on her," Maurizio said dryly. "She didn't marry him for love. She set a high price on herself and he was fool enough to pay it. But she didn't keep her side of the bargain. She's nervous and she has reason to be." He saw Terri's shocked eyes. "Don't look like that. These marriage deals are done all the time."

"But not by—" Terri began fiercely and checked herself, dismayed at how close she'd come to a disastrous revelation. Something bitter and disturbing in Maurizio's voice had brought her to the edge of defending the mother who was a stranger to her.

"Not by?" He was regarding her closely.

"Not—not by every woman," Terri said hastily.

"I wonder if that was really what you were going to say."

"If you want to know what I'm really thinking," she said crossly, "I don't like the way you talked about her. You think you know what she's like but you don't really. Nobody knows that much about another person."

"Are you angry with me, Teresa?" He sounded surprised.

"Yes, I am. You sounded so *cruel*. As though it pleased you to think of her misfortune."

"Aren't you also judging me too easily?" Maurizio asked, an edge to his voice. "What do you know of me that you call me cruel?"

"I think you could be very cruel when it suited you," Terri said in a voice of discovery. "I think there's something cruel about this very room."

"What on earth are you talking about?"

"The mirrors all around the walls...they're all distorted. It makes everyone look slightly diabolical."

Maurizio flushed. "The mirrors are antiques," he said. "Such distortions are common in mirrors of that age. If you're suggesting that I planned it this way, you are wrong." To his intense annoyance, he realized that he was defending himself, something foreign to his nature. "If you must know," he added, "I hadn't even noticed the distortions."

It was true. He'd been so proud of decorating the casino with priceless antiques that he'd failed to observe the slight imperfection. But her clear eyes had seen it at once, and now this room would never be quite the same to him. He had an almost childish feeling of disappointment, as though she'd spoiled his treasure.

At that moment, the Calvanis appeared in the entrance at the far end. They were still too far away for Terri to make out details, but she could see that they were a beautiful couple. Francisco was handsome and distinguished, with dark hair, graying at the sides. Elena was graceful and slender. Her dress clung to her delicate curves as if it had been molded to them, and the plunging neckline revealed the swell of high, firm breasts. As she entered the room with a languid, sauntering gait, she was the object of admiration, and the way she looked neither to the right nor the left suggested that she knew it.

Terri knew a moment of disappointment. Elena was undoubtedly a beautiful woman but she wasn't Terri's idea of a mother. Then Leo's words came back to her. "I was disappointed at first," he'd said when he called home to describe his first meeting with Elena. "She seemed too young to be our mother. But when you look into her eyes—she's magic, so kind and sweet."

Maurizio led Terri toward them. "Francisco, Elena," he said with professional affability. "Nice to see you here again. The party is never complete without you. Allow me to introduce Signorina Teresa Wainright."

Terri's eyes were fixed on Elena intently enough to catch the faint frisson that passed over her features. It was barely perceptible, little more than a variation of stillness, but it was there on the lovely face that looked on her daughter for the first time. Of course, she was reacting to Leo's surname, Terri thought. That was all. As far as she knew, Leo had never revealed his true identity to Elena.

Someone else was also watching Elena for her reaction. Maurizio's eyes were hard as he studied her, missing nothing, noting the brief silence before she smiled and said graciously, "It's a pleasure to meet you, *signorina*."

"Indeed it is," Francisco seconded at once. "A friend of Maurizio's is a friend of ours." He took Terri's hand and bent low to touch it with his lips. It was an elegant gesture, smooth, practiced and almost meaningless. But when he raised his head, a change had come over him. His eyes on Terri had suddenly become as hard as Maurizio's, lit from deep within by a cold, appraising gleam.

"You must join me for some champagne," Maurizio said, guiding them to a little bay, slightly apart from the main room.

"Have you been in Venice for very long, *signorina?*" Francisco inquired politely when they were seated around a low table.

"Only a day."

"You're here on vacation?"

"Partly," Terri responded cautiously. "I work as an Italian translator and I thought I should see something of the country."

"You've chosen a strange time to come to Venice. Winter is drawing near and the tourists are going home."

"Yes, I saw that a great many of the hotels were closed, but the Midas seems busy enough."

"The luxury hotels are full all the year," Francisco said. "When the tourists go, the business conventions arrive. Fortunately, although the conferences fill the expensive hotels, they leave the streets fairly uncluttered. We Venetians like to have our city to ourselves again."

"Yes, I should think all those people tramping over it must hide the city," Terri responded. "I haven't had a chance to see much, but it must be fascinating when it's quiet.''

Francisco looked at her with new interest. ''Hide the city,'' he echoed. ''That's exactly how I feel. They come in their millions to see Venice, and all they see is one another. Welcome to my city, *signorina*. I'm glad that you'll see it at its best.''

Terri looked across at Elena who'd been listening to this conversation. ''And you, Contessa? Do you like Venice best at this time of year?''

''No,'' Elena admitted with a little shudder. ''In winter it seems to me to be a sinister place, full of shades and dark corners.''

''You're being fanciful, my dear,'' Francisco told her coolly. ''You see shades where there are none.''

''Perhaps it's because the *contessa* is an artist,'' Maurizio said. ''Artists are always a little fanciful.''

''I own an art gallery in this city,'' Francisco explained to Terri. ''My wife supervises it very ably.''

''And I'm sure you've done the *contessa* an injustice,'' Terri told Maurizio. ''You don't have to be fanciful to be an artist. My brother is artistic, and through him I've met several artists. Most of them struck me as very tough and practical.''

''That's true,'' Elena agreed, smiling at her as if grateful for the young woman's support. ''The artists I deal with all seem to have eyes like hawks for the last penny. Or their agents do.''

''I'm sure you deal with them very efficiently, my dear,'' Francisco said. ''Your own ability to spot the last penny has frequently earned my respect.''

It was said with a smile and might just have passed for a compliment. But there was something faintly disagreeable about Francisco's manner that chilled

Terri. It seemed that Elena felt the same because a wan smile crossed her face.

Guests were arriving fast. Maurizio toasted the trio in champagne before excusing himself. Elena's attention was immediately claimed by several men at once and she vanished in an eager group, leaving Terri with Francisco. "Do you play?" he asked.

"I'm not a gambler," she confessed with a laugh. "I played for the first time tonight, using the complimentary chips we were all given."

"Ah, yes. How clever of Maurizio to do that. Of course, he knows he'll get it all back with interest before the evening's over."

Terri realized this was true, but something in Francisco's arrogant manner made her feel like being contrary. "Perhaps he won't. Some people do get lucky."

"One or two," Francisco conceded with a shrug. "But overall, the casino always emerges the winner. To be more precise, Maurizio is always the winner—in play and in life. He makes sure of that."

"In play and in life," Terri echoed.

"No man in Venice is more ruthless or more feared. Has nobody told you that?"

"No."

He laughed. "Well, you'll discover it for yourself."

"Why are you trying to turn me against him?"

"But I'm not. I'm a Venetian and so is he. Venetians respect exactly those qualities that have made Maurizio what he is." With a smooth gesture, he lifted a glass of champagne from a passing tray and handed it to her. "Why don't we take a little fresh air?" he said, indicating the terrace.

A ripple of laughter from behind them made Terri turn her head. Elena was in the center of a group of admirers, laughing merrily, and she looked as if she didn't have a care in the world. "She's so beautiful," Terri said wistfully.

"Yes, indeed. Everybody says so," Francisco agreed. "Sometimes I have to compete for her attention. I'm a proud—though somewhat neglected—husband." But he didn't sound proud.

"I'm sure she doesn't really neglect you," Terri said.

"But of course she does. Husbands and wives ought to neglect each other. To live in each other's pockets would be very boring. A few—how shall I put it delicately?—'outside interests' add spice to a marriage." He laughed. "Have I shocked you?"

"Of course not," she disclaimed hastily, feeling gauche and provincial. She was less shocked than embarrassed by the feeling that Francisco was deliberately *trying* to shock her. Glancing up, she saw that he was watching her in a way that made her uncomfortable. She became intensely aware of how provocatively she was dressed, not pleasantly aware as with Maurizio, but as though she were revealing something to Francisco's sharp eyes that ought to be kept hidden.

"I visited England once," Francisco said. "I found Englishwomen intriguing. They say one thing, look another and mean something entirely different."

"That's the only way to keep men on their toes," Terri responded lightly.

He gave her an amused flirtatious smile. "How right you are. And what would life be if women always said what they thought?"

"Are you on that subject again?" a musical voice asked behind them. Countess Elena had detached herself from the crowd and swayed gracefully onto the terrace to join them. "Don't let him bore you, *signorina*. Francisco never believes that *anyone* means what they say or says what they mean."

"I've found very few people who can be relied on," her husband replied, his eyes fixed on his wife.

The words were spoken lightly enough, but again Terri sensed the tension between husband and wife. The next moment, she'd forgotten Francisco as Elena turned the full beam of her charm on her. "So you've never gambled before tonight? Then you must gamble with me. I'm lucky. Everybody says so."

Brooking no refusal, she took Terri's hand and led her firmly to the nearest roulette table. Several men cheered and made way for her as she approached, but some of them had curious eyes for Terri, too.

Elena played according to what she called her method, but as far as Terri could make out, it was simply chance dressed up to look like logic. Elena would stake a number because the fancy took her and invent a multitude of reasons for her choice afterward. Once, she actually won, then proceeded to lose every chip trying to repeat the trick. She greeted triumph and disaster with the same merry laugh. "I don't think you really care whether you win or lose," Terri said.

Elena shrugged. "True. What difference does it make? In fact," she added, looking around her at the noisy throng, "what difference does anything make?" She sighed. "I envy you for being English."

"Envy me? Why?"

"The English are serious. They know what matters and what doesn't. I used to think it was terrible to be serious, but now—" She shrugged.

Terri was intrigued by her. Elena seemed to have a different mood for every moment. If only she could get her alone for a real talk!

But there seemed no chance of it. Terri began to feel apprehensive as the night slipped away without her achieving anything.

Elena gave a brittle laugh. "Now I don't know what I think, or why I'm talking like this."

"You're tired, my dear," Francisco said, appearing at her side.

"Yes," Elena agreed. "And I'm even more tired when I think of all I have to do tomorrow. So many letters to write and phone calls to make."

"Perhaps you need a secretary," Terri suggested.

"I have one—or rather I had. Denise is French and very efficient, but a few weeks ago she had to go and nurse her sick mother. I promised to keep the job open, but while she's gone I don't know what to do."

"Employ someone for a short time only," Francisco said. To Terri he added, "As well as having an—interesting—social life, my wife is involved in many charity works, plus the art gallery. Some form of organization is imperative."

Terri's heart was hammering. Out of the blue it seemed she was being offered the chance of her dreams. "I wonder if I might be allowed to help," she ventured. "I need to do some work when I'm in Venice, and I'm very organized."

Maurizio had appeared in time to hear the last part of the conversation. He was standing strangely still, as though his life depended on the words he was hearing. To Terri's surprise, he frowned. "I don't think you should rush to do this," he said. "The *contessa*'s work covers a wide area. It needs someone who's familiar with this country, and especially with Venice."

"I disagree," Francisco said. "I believe Signorina Wainright would be an excellent choice, and so does my wife."

"Of course," Elena said. She was still smiling but there was a strange quenched air about her, as though a light had gone out. And suddenly Terri knew that Elena was afraid of her husband.

"Look," she said quickly, "forget I suggested it. I shouldn't have embarrassed you like that. Maurizio is quite right."

"But please, I want you," Elena said. She'd regained her composure and managed a warm smile. "I need you to keep me in order."

"So it's an arrangement that suits everybody," Francisco said, ignoring Maurizio's scowl. "You can move into our house tomorrow *signorina*."

"Move in?" She was startled.

"Why live at the Midas when you can live with us for nothing?" Francisco asked. "It makes no sense."

"I think it makes no sense for you to live with your employers until you've learned whether you all suit one another," Maurizio said. "Don't rush into this, Teresa."

"You're right," she agreed. "I'd like to take the job, but it's better if I continue to live here just now."

Francisco shrugged. "As you please. My only thought was for your comfort." He spoke coldly, as if he'd taken offense at having his suggestion rejected.

The party was breaking up. Maurizio's attention was occupied in bidding goodbye to people. The Calvanis were making preparations to leave. Elena suddenly seized Terri's hands in both of hers. "You'll come to me tomorrow," she said, "and we—we will be very well together," she finished in a hurry.

Francisco offered Elena his arm and inclined his head toward Terri. As she returned the salutation, Terri became aware that he was watching her with a strange expression in his cold, hard eyes. It was watchful and appraising, yet held a curious, unpleasant kind of satisfaction. She gave him a polite smile and watched with relief as he escorted his wife away.

In spite of her discomfiture over Francisco, she was in a delighted daze at the chance to get so close to Elena. She glanced across at Maurizio but he was knee-deep in people and plainly wouldn't be free for some time. She caught his eye long enough to smile a good-night, and left.

The Calvanis made the return journey to their palazzo in silence. Nor did they look at each other. There had been no quarrel. This was their normal behavior.

As soon as they reached home, a servant murmured a message to Francisco, who received it with a slight note of dismissal. "My mother wishes to see me before I retire," he informed his wife. "Perhaps you, too, would like to pay her your respects?"

"You know better than to think I'd like to do any such thing," Elena observed wearily. "Nor does your mother truly wish it. She detests me."

"Then oblige me by doing this because *I* wish it," Francisco said firmly.

Elena shrugged and fell into step beside him on the stairs. "Very well. Although why you should insist on us all going through this farce, I can't imagine."

"I'm sure you can't," he replied. "A woman of my own background would have understood that some proprieties have to be maintained without needing it explained to her.''

Elena winced, as though years of such snubs hadn't blunted their power to wound her. A small pleased smile was her husband's only response. Together they made their way to the apartment of Lisa, the old *contessa*.

She greeted them sitting up in a huge, old-fashioned bed, where she spent most of her time. She was eighty, extremely thin and had been a semiofficial invalid ever since collapsing a week before her son's wedding eighteen years ago. Anxious doctors had treated her for heart trouble, nerve trouble and anything else they could think of, but none of them had dared voice what all knew to be the truth, that Francisco's mother was suffering from a severe bout of displeasure at her son's choice of bride. It had persisted until the present day.

Reclining on satin, lace-edged pillows, she watched the approach of her son and daughter-in-law. Her sharp eyes missed nothing, including Elena's smile, held on by willpower. "You're looking well, Mama," Elena said brightly. "I hope that means you're feeling better."

"I'm as well as I ever am," Lisa informed her sourly. "My visitors exhausted me, but one has one's obligations."

"I'm glad you had company, Mama," Francisco observed. "Who was it?"

"Antonio brought his new wife to visit me. Such a pleasure to meet her. Only four months married and pregnant already, which is exactly right. The first child should always be secured quickly, especially when there is a great inheritance to be considered."

"I just came in to say good-night," Elena said in a strained voice. "I won't stay. I'm rather tired."

"Good night," Lisa responded distantly, presenting her cheek for Elena's dutiful kiss. She waited until Elena had departed, then turned to look at her son. A significant glance passed between them. "How much longer will you allow this to go on?" she demanded in a rough voice that contrasted with her frail appearance. "You're fifty-five and time is running out. Where are your sons? Why aren't you doing something to get them?"

"You make it sound so easy, Mama, but things are complicated."

"Nonsense. You've got to get rid of her, and quickly. Doesn't she give you any excuse?"

"Unfortunately no. My wife is infuriatingly discreet. She has occasional romances, but she never goes beyond playing the kind of games all society plays."

"Surely there must have been more?"

Francisco shrugged. "There was one young man a few months ago, during Carnival, but nothing came of it."

"You've been clumsy. She knows you're watching her, so of course she's discreet. Well, it's your own fault. I warned you against marrying her but you wouldn't listen. You were hot to get her into your bed, she held out for marriage and like a fool you capitulated."

Francisco gave a wintry smile. "I believe you caught by father by much the same methods."

Lisa cackled. "Yes, but on the wedding night, he was rewarded for his patience. Was your Elena worth waiting for?"

"You know very well that she wasn't," Francisco said coldly. "All that waiting, putting me off, all that exaggerated modesty. She seemed to be made of ice, and acted as though the sight of a man would make her swoon. And what did I find? It was all a cynical performance to fool me. She'd already been with a man."

"You should have got rid of her then."

"It's easy to say that now," Francisco told her irritably, "but she never admitted it, and I had no idea who to suspect. A man she knew in England probably. Even then she could have redeemed herself by giving me a son. But she's barren, and the years are hurrying by."

Lisa took his arm with a clawlike grip. "Be careful that she doesn't dismiss *you.* Your 'hobbies' are too well-known, and unlike your wife, you're not always discreet."

"I don't know what you mean."

Lisa made a sound of exasperation. "Don't pretend with me. I lived too many years with your father to be deluded. His favorite pastime was debauchery of the young and innocent—and the younger and more innocent, the more he enjoyed it. It was my fate to bear him a son who's his mirror image. And I know how many little 'unofficial' Calvanis there are in this city."

Francisco shrugged. "At least there's no doubt that it is my wife, not I, who's barren." He strode restlessly about the room, pausing at last before an ornate gilt mirror that reflected the room behind him, and his mother, dominating everything from her huge bed, like a spider. "Young and innocent," he mused.

"An ice maiden. That's how I saw her—that's what she made me believe she was—and all the time—"

"Enough," Lisa said imperiously. "It's useless to dwell on the past. What you need now is a wife that can give you sons. Forget about ice maidens, or keep them for your fantasies. In real life they don't exist."

"Now, there you're wrong, Mama," Francisco said, speaking to her in the mirror. "They do exist, and I think—yes, I really think I've met one."

Later that night, Francisco stopped outside his wife's room. Putting his ear to the door, he listened to a muffled noise coming from within. After a moment, he quietly turned the handle and opened the door a crack. Now he could clearly hear the sound of violent sobbing coming from Elena's bed. The hardest heart might have been touched by those sobs with their message of anguish suppressed for too long, of wretchedness hidden by a brilliant smile, of an aching, desperate loneliness.

After listening for a moment longer, Francisco grunted, closed the door and went away.

Chapter Five

The Palazzo Calvani lay at the opposite end of Venice to the Midas Hotel, around the huge bend of the Grand Canal. On the first day, Maurizio escorted her onto the vaporetto, the big water bus that plied its way slowly along the canal, stopping on alternate sides.

"You didn't wait for me last night," he reproached her as they stood in the boat, watching the ancient buildings slip by.

"You were going to be hours with your guests, otherwise I'd have waited," she said. "There was something I wanted to say."

"Yes?" He leaned his head close to her.

"Why did you try to stop me from taking this marvelous job?"

Maurizio made a wry face as if reluctantly appreciating a joke at his own expense. "Was that all you wanted to say to me?"

"Of course."

He sighed. "Of course."

"It's important. The *contessa* knew Leo. If I can be close to her day by day, I may learn something of his whereabouts."

"Just be careful."

"Careful? Of what?"

"Say rather of whom. Francisco Calvani is—" He hesitated. "Well, anyway, be careful."

"You speak of him much as he speaks of you," she said, amused. "He said you were always the winner, in play and in life."

"Damn his nerve!"

"Isn't it true?" she asked, looking up at him merrily. This morning she wanted to sing with joy for no other reason than that he was here, with her, giving her all his attention.

Maurizio didn't answer at first. He was looking into her face, trying to believe that this natural, laughing young woman with the breeze in her hair was the same person as the cool siren who'd driven him wild the day before. Did she know how many men's eyes had followed her in the roulette room? Did she care? Or did she think only of her brother?

"What—what did you say?" he asked, aware that his wits were wandering.

"I said, is it true?"

"Is what true?"

"You're not listening to a word I say."

No, he thought. *I'm not listening to your words but I can't take my eyes from your mouth and the delightful way it moves, especially when you smile. In another moment, I shall yield to temptation and kiss you in public. What's happening to me? When did I go mad?*

"I said, is it true that you're always the winner?"

He gathered his wits. "No, that's just what I want people to believe."

"He also said that no one in Venice was more ruthless or more feared. But I didn't believe that."

"Why not?" he asked quickly.

"I don't know. I just ... don't." She felt awkward. The conversation was suddenly too intimate and revealing.

"I wonder who knows me best, Teresa. Francisco or you?"

"Why does he say such things of you?"

He shrugged. "I could say the same of him. We're old enemies."

"But why?"

"We're Venetians. Enmity is natural. This is our landing stage."

He alighted with her. As they neared the palazzo Francisco was just stepping into his motorboat. He glanced up, saw them and immediately came up the steps. "What a pleasure to see you, *signorina*," he said. "My wife will be delighted. Maurizio, do you wish to come inside for a moment?" He didn't sound enthusiastic.

"Thank you, no," Maurizio said. "I must return to work."

He vanished into the rabbit warren of streets and Francisco led Terri inside. The next moment Elena had appeared at the top of a flight of stairs and was hurrying down to enfold her in a scented embrace. Francisco melted away, leaving his wife to take charge of

Terri and draw her upstairs to the *contessa*'s private apartments.

Last night, in the soft lights of the casino, Elena had looked little more than a girl. In the brilliant morning sunshine, Terri could see signs of strain, and even a slight redness, as though Elena had been weeping. But then she smiled, the strain vanished and the illusion of youth was almost restored. Although it was early in the day, Elena was perfectly and glossily groomed, with elegantly coiffured hair and flawlessly applied makeup.

Terri's Italian blood spoke up for Elena in tones of warm admiration, but she'd been reared as an Englishwoman and something puritanical in her looked askance at a woman who gave so much attention and energy to her own appearance. She knew what Elena had sacrificed to become the gorgeous Contessa Calvani. So in her heart she stood a little aside, even while part of her succumbed to Elena's charm.

"Contessa, I'm afraid I was foisted on you," Terri said impulsively. "I really hope I can make you glad I'm here."

"But I'm glad already," Elena said warmly. "I have so much to do and I'm so scatterbrained. Look at all this." She indicated a beautiful marquetry desk covered with papers. "They built up while I was away, and now I must go through them all."

"Then the sooner we start the better," Terri said.

By the end of the first day, Terri had changed her mind about Elena. She was far from scatterbrained, and worked with a brisk efficiency that covered a lot of ground in a short time. She divided her time into three: her charity work, the art gallery and the considerable effort of maintaining her position as a society dazzler. At first, her charity work appeared impersonal, a matter of committees and fund-raising events. But then, she spent nearly two hours on the telephone arguing for the rights of a disabled child, refusing to give up until the child was given a government grant Elena felt he deserved. Her last call was to his mother to announce gleefully, "We won." She was like a child herself, enjoying an unexpected present, and Terri, who'd heard her harrying officials unmercifully, was intrigued at the many-sided personality unfolding before her.

They lunched at the art gallery where Elena criticized her assistant for a piece of mismanagement while she'd been away, but sweetened her reproof with a smile that brought him back under her spell. "I thought he was going to walk out at first," Terri observed when the man had left the office. "But you had him wagging his tail like a puppy."

"Of course." Elena shrugged. "I don't like to hurt people, even when I have to be cross with them." She glanced at Terri. "What are you looking at?"

Terri lifted some drawings that were lying in a tray. "I thought I recognized my brother's hand."

"Your brother?"

"Leo Wainright. I believe he did some work for you here?"

"Yes—yes, he did. Of course, you mentioned a brother...."

"And he really did work here? You knew him?"

Elena unlocked a small cabinet and took out some jewelry. "This piece is about four hundred years old and I'm afraid it's falling to pieces. The stones need resetting, and Leo and I were going to do it together. Those drawings are his initial designs. I thought they were so beautiful, but one day he must have lost interest because he never came back to finish work."

"When was that?"

"Late September, I think. Did he ever tell why he didn't return?"

"I haven't heard from him since then," Terri said. She kept her voice casual as she repeated her prepared story. "He always liked not knowing what was going to happen tomorrow, so he'd jaunt off without telling anyone where he was going. But I know he loved Italy, so I thought I'd come out to see if I liked it, too."

"Yes, Leo was very happy-go-lucky," Elena agreed with a touch of relief. "He'd forget appointments—but it didn't mean anything. Did it?"

"Not a thing," Terri agreed cheerfully. She didn't want to frighten Elena. Nothing would be achieved by that.

The latter part of the afternoon was taken up by a visit to Vilani, Elena's dressmaker, because the *contessa* had discovered that her winter wardrobe was too small. She was an exacting customer and Terri spent two hours taking notes of her detailed requirements so that these could later be compared with what Vilani produced. This was accomplished with shrewd efficiency concealed behind a seemingly vague charm. There was a lot more to Elena than met the eye.

They returned to the palazzo to have cake and a glass of sparkling white wine. Then Elena went off to take a nap, in preparation for an evening of gaiety, and Terri bid her goodbye. As she was crossing the hall Francisco appeared and hailed her. "Before you leave, *signorina,* perhaps you will do me a small favor."

"Of course, if I can."

"My mother would like to meet you. She's bedridden and never leaves her own apartments. It's easy for her to feel left out of things. She would greatly appreciate your going to visit her."

"Of course. I should be delighted."

He led her up two floors, knocked and stood waiting until a cool voice said, "Enter."

Terri's first impression of the old *contessa* was that she was enthroned. She lay in the center of a huge bed, propped up by satin pillows. Above her head was a canopy, gathered up into a coronet. The occupant of the bed was tiny and birdlike, yet she easily dominated everything in the room. Terri had to resist the desire to curtsy.

"Signorina Wainright has come to pay her respects to you, Mama," Francisco declared.

The little hand that clasped Terri's was strong despite its delicacy, and the *contessa* pulled her down until she was sitting on the bed. "How kind," she said. "I see so few people. Let me take a better look at you." She raised a lorgnette and studied her visitor as if Terri were a creature under a microscope. Terri was a bit put out, but clearly this old woman felt free from the code of manners that governed lesser mortals. "Very nice," she said at last. "Tell me about yourself, young woman. My son says you are English."

Terri gave her a few carefully chosen and unrevealing details. It sounded bland and dull to her own ears but the old woman nodded as if satisfied. "How long do you plan to stay in Italy?" she asked at last.

"I don't know. It might be some time."

"And your family? Don't they mind?"

"I have no family except my brother, and he, too, is traveling in Italy."

A cynical smile flickered across the *contessa*'s face. "But surely you have a lover somewhere at home? You modern young women all have lovers."

Trying not to be embarrassed, Terri said, "I have no lover."

"I don't believe you," the *contessa* said bluntly. "You're so pretty, you must have a lover."

"But I don't," Terri said, definitely disliking her now. "I guess I'm just not very modern."

"So it would seem. Well, I don't like you the worse for it."

"Thank you," Terri said, trying to keep the irony out of her voice.

Suddenly, the old *contessa* cackled. "You don't care whether I like you or not. No, don't deny it. Good for you. But don't be *too* independent, will you? I can be a good friend. I could even show you how to achieve great things."

"You're very kind," Terri said, wondering what on earth the old woman was talking about.

The *contessa* lay back wearily against her pillows. "You'd better leave now," she said.

Francisco showed her down to the front door. "Forgive my mother's abrupt manners," he said. "She belongs to another generation, another world."

"Please don't think anything of it," Terri begged.

"I knew I could rely on your kindness. I think you're a very understanding person, *signorina*. I was sure of it from the first moment."

Terri murmured something polite, but she was longing to escape. As she descended the stairs, a surprise awaited her. Maurizio was standing in the hall below.

"I had business in this part of town," he explained. "I thought I'd escort you home in case you get lost."

"There was no danger of that," Francisco said. "I was about to send Signorina Wainright home in my own boat."

"You're all consideration, Count," Maurizio responded smoothly. "Fortunately, it won't be necessary."

He stood back while Terri passed outside, then followed her. Then he bid Francisco good-night, and closed the door. Francisco stood looking at the door, his face a cold, expressionless mask. After a moment, he turned and went slowly back upstairs to his mother's room. "Well?" he demanded.

The old *contessa* nodded. "This time your instinct is excellent," she said. "She will do very well."

"You're cold," Maurizio said when they'd walked a little way. "Perhaps we should take the boat."

"No," Terri said quickly. A boat would get them home too quickly. She wanted to enjoy this time with Maurizio.

"Let's have a coffee, then."

He took her into a small café. The man serving grinned and greeted him by name. Maurizio responded, addressing him as Giorgio. "He knows you," Terri exclaimed.

"Why are you so surprised?"

"It's just not the sort of place I associate with you. It's not a bit like the Midas."

"When I was sixteen years old, and very poor, I boarded here with Giorgio and his wife. They didn't charge me anything. I earned my keep by serving in the

evenings and cleaning up when the customers had
gone home. They're kind people and I was happy—or
rather I would have been happy if I hadn't been am-
bitious. Every night before I went to sleep, I would
promise myself that for me Venice would one day be
a city of gold. I would be like King Midas, making
gold of everything I touched.''

"And you succeeded," Terri said, hoping he would
continue.

"Yes, I succeeded." He made a face.

"But you're still not happy. Losing Rufio spoiled
everything for you."

"Gold is nothing without someone to share it
with," he agreed quietly.

"Was Rufio with you then?"

"Yes. Giorgio's wife used to care for him with her
own children during the day, but he slept in my room.
I used to confide all my dreams and ambitions to him.
He didn't think I was crazy, like everyone else did. He
was two years old and we understood each other.

"When at last I made money, I could give him all
the things I would have liked when I was his age. I
suppose I spoiled him, but he never *became* spoilt. He
never lost his sweet temper or his faith in people. He
believed that the world was good—" Maurizio
checked himself abruptly.

"Then to him it *was* good," Terri said gently, pity-
ing his pain.

"He is *dead*. Did a good world do that to him?"

She shook her head. There was no answer. "How
did he die?"

"He committed suicide. If you've finished, we
should be going."

She followed him out of the café in silence. After a while, he slipped an arm around her shoulder. "I'm an ill-tempered bear," he said remorsefully.

"I should be sorry for prying."

"You weren't prying. It's me. I have no manners." He looked down and suddenly tightened his arm and kissed her. "What is it?" he asked as he felt her stiffen.

"People will see us."

"Is that bad? In Venice, people kiss in public all the time. I believe it even happens in chilly England."

"Perhaps, but the English don't approve of it," she said, remembering Madge.

"But you aren't English. You're Italian, and it's about time you learned to approve of it," he responded firmly, tightening his arm again.

Her head began to spin, almost enough to overcome her embarrassment. The touch of his lips was magic and the magic became part of her, spreading right through her until she was humming with pleasure from head to foot. If only she could be alone with him, there was so much more she wanted. "Maurizio, please—not here—"

His eyes were alight with laughter, something she hadn't seen before, and her heart turned over. "Maurizio—"

"Wait," he said, covering her mouth once more. "When I've kissed you again, we'll talk—if anything's that important."

Nothing was that important, she realized. Nothing in the world mattered but being in his arms, holding him closely. And with that realization came alarm. No other man had ever brought her so close to throwing caution to the winds. And in public. *Slut. Slut.*

"No, please," she protested breathlessly. "Not here, not now."

To her relief, he released her. "When and where then?" he said. The demon of mischief was still in his eyes.

"I think we should be going home," she said rather breathlessly.

Instantly he stopped and leaned against the wall. "But I want to remain here," he said, grinning.

"Then I'll return to the Midas alone."

"Do you think you can do it without getting lost?"

"Watch me." She slipped away around the corner and darted into a souvenir shop. The window was crowded with a display of goods and she was able to hide behind it, peering through a small gap between two masks. After a moment, she saw Maurizio appear around the corner and stand scratching his head, staring down the street. To Terri's delight, he ran to the far end, glanced in both directions and returned, looking worried.

When he dived into a café on the other side, she took pity on him and emerged, positioning herself by the café door and leaning against the wall in an exact imitation of his earlier pose. When he hurried out, she laughed. "If you're lost, perhaps I can show you the way home," she offered when he turned to see her.

"You little wretch," he said in exasperation. Then the ire disappeared from his eyes as he saw her teasing expression. He put his hands on the wall, one on each side of her. "So you want to play games, do you? I can't afford to spend time like this. I have work to do."

"Then why are you here?"

The question echoed in his brain. Why was he here being entranced by her mischief when he had serious things to attend to? Every moment that he let her cast her spell on him was a betrayal of Rufio.

"Why am I here?" he repeated. "I don't know. We should have been home minutes ago."

The moment was over. Terri watched as something died in his eyes, leaving them blank and unreadable. Without another word, she took the arm he offered and let him lead her home.

Over the next three weeks, Terri became part of life in the palazzo. Elena relied on her totally, and often asked her to remain in the evenings to help out with the many parties she gave. Because of these extra duties exacted of Terri, she gave her a generous dress allowance and told her to shop with Vilani. Terri's wardrobe quickly grew more extensive and more glamorous, and she looked less and less like her old self.

If Francisco was at home, he would join them for coffee in the afternoon and make serious attempts to engage her in conversation. These were seldom successful because Terri felt awkward with him, but he didn't seem to mind. Often she would look up and find his eyes fixed on her as though he were sizing her up for some purpose. She reflected that he was an art dealer and this was probably his manner of looking at everyone, but it made her uncomfortable.

Occasionally, she would be summoned by the old *contessa,* and their conversation would follow the same pattern as at their first meeting. The old woman would ask personal questions in her sharp voice and seem satisfied with the answers. Afterward, Francisco, who was always present, would apologize but assure Terri how much his mother really liked her. "She sees great possibilities in you," he said once. "I wonder if you've realized that."

"Well—no," Terri replied awkwardly.

"No, of course not. It's part of your charm, *signorina,* to be unaware of the effect you have on others."

She was summoned again two days later, and this time she displeased the countess. "I don't understand why you're still living at the Midas," the old woman said. "You should be staying here. Francisco, see to it."

"Signorina Wainright has her own ideas about that, Mama," her son said with a smile that didn't quite reach his eyes.

"I prefer to remain at the Midas," Terri said.

"Nonsense. It isn't a suitable place for a young woman. You must come here at once."

"I think not," Terri said firmly.

"What did you say?"

"You're very kind but I don't consider it a good idea to live and work in the same building."

The old *contessa*'s eyes narrowed. "At one time, if I had deigned to show my friendship to a young woman, moreover a young woman without background or lineage, whose prospects would otherwise be—"

"That was in the past, Mama," Francisco interrupted quickly. "These days, young women are independent." A look passed between him and his mother, almost as if he was warning her about something. "We can discuss this another time." Then, he hurried Terri out of the room.

"What difference does it make to your mother where I live?" Terri demanded wrathfully as they went downstairs.

"I'm afraid she's rather domineering. She likes to have people where she can bully them. Please forgive her."

"Very well, but I don't think I ought to visit her again if I'm just going to make her angry."

"Oh, but she likes you very much. You must believe that. Not everyone wins my mother's favor. My wife, I'm afraid, was quite unable to do so, which is a pity. But that favor isn't something to be lightly thrown away."

Terri made some polite response and escaped. She disliked both Francisco and his mother and couldn't see why she should be expected to be pleased at such "favor." She meant to ask Elena about their curious attitude, but the next day a crisis blew up at the art gallery and in the chaos she forgot all about it.

One evening, she stayed to help Elena with a late-afternoon charity function that went on until nine o'clock. When it was over, Francisco tried to insist on taking her home in his motorboat, but she managed to evade him, and slipped away before he could think of more arguments.

She knew the way home by now and enjoyed exploring the shops on the route. Most of them were closed at this hour, but one souvenir shop had gamely stayed open, and on impulse she went in, drawn by the huge array of masks that hung all over the walls: full face and half face; plain white and multicoloured; masks of normal faces and masks with enormously elongated noses. She took down a clown's mask and tried it on. It covered her face completely and she was regarding herself in the mirror with fascination when a cheerful voice said, "Good evening, Teresa," and there stood Bruno, smiling at her. She laughed.

"You weren't supposed to know it was me," she protested, removing the mask.

"Of course I knew," he said at once. "There are some people that nothing can disguise because they're so much themselves. You're one of those people."

"But you don't know me."

"Don't I? Well, perhaps. And perhaps I know you better than Maurizio, who thinks he knows everything."

She was going to ask what he meant by this but Bruno was going through the masks as eagerly as a child. "Look at them," he said happily. "How I look forward to Carnival, the time of anarchy and lawlessness. Now *that's* the true spirit of Venice."

"I thought the spirit of Venice was supposed to be love," Terri teased.

"And what is more lawless than love?" he demanded cryptically. "Does passion choose its object with an eye to propriety and convenience? Certainly not. Since passion obeys no laws, it's the ultimate and most beautiful anarchy."

There was a rare light in his eyes, making her realize that Bruno's frail body, much abused by tobacco and alcohol, had also been shaken by beautiful anarchy, and he would seek it again as long as he had strength. "Long live anarchy!" he declared, reading comprehension in her face.

"Long live love," she replied.

"If you wish. At your age, one believes in love. At my age—let's say that a lifetime's experience has taught me about masks."

"You mean that lovers are always playing parts and wearing masks?" she hazarded.

"It goes deeper than that. Long ago, people believed that if you donned a mask, you weren't pretending to be another person—you actually *became* that person. Think of it! The power to *be* anyone you liked, and then be someone else—the variety of life, the old scores you could settle, the love affairs you could enjoy. Ah, think of it!" His expression was radiant and Terri smiled. She was deeply fond of Bruno and she wondered if perhaps he reminded her a little of her father. Not in looks, but in a gleam of memory she'd sometimes seen in Carlo's eyes without understanding it. He, too, had known beautiful anarchy and had never been the same again.

"What is it?" Bruno asked quickly.

"Nothing. Why?"

"You sighed."

"Did I? I didn't notice. Tell me more about the masks. What do they all represent?"

If Bruno noticed her quickly covering her tracks, he didn't mention it. "Some of them are based on the old commedia dell'arte characters," he said, beginning to hold them up. "Harlequin, part devil, part clown. Columbine, his female counterpart but far more cunning. Pulcinella, who comes from the underworld. Pantalone, the old merchant. Or these, covered in tinsel and sequins, which a pretty lady can use to conceal her interest in a man while keeping him under observation."

With a swift movement, Bruno gathered up a dozen masks and indicated to the hovering assistant that he would buy them. A few moments later, he was carrying them out of the shop, one arm around Terri's shoulders, talking ceaselessly as he guided her through the streets.

"Just wait until you see Carnival," he said. "Hundreds of years ago, the wearing of disguises was forbidden because they made it so easy for criminals to escape detection. The law was relaxed during Carnival, so for those few days everyone went crazy."

He steered her into Giorgio's café, sat her down and bought her a coffee. For himself, he obtained a bottle of red wine, which he proceeded to consume at an alarming rate. "The owners here are friends of Maurizio's," he observed.

"I know. He brought me here once before. He told me he boarded out with them years ago, and they were very kind to him."

"He's returned the kindness a hundredfold. When Giorgio got into financial difficulties a few years back, Maurizio simply bought the café and made them a present of it."

"He didn't tell me that."

"He wouldn't. Maurizio never tells anyone about himself if he can help it."

"He's told me a little—about Rufio."

Bruno regarded her curiously and for a moment he didn't speak.

There was something strange about him, Terri reflected, as though he didn't really belong here or anywhere. He was like the clown-devil Harlequin, jumping into situations, staying just long enough to say something illuminating, then jumping out again. But there was kindness in that cynical, battered face, and she felt instinctively that she could trust him.

At last Bruno said, "If Maurizio has talked about Rufio, then he's allowed you close to his heart. It's very strange that—" He checked himself.

"Strange that what?"

"Nothing. I'm only his uncle. I don't really understand him at all."

"Did you know him when he was living here?"

"Slightly. I wasn't in Venice much. I kept having to leave to escape various people—creditors, angry husbands, that sort of thing." His gesture implied a whole world of outraged authority, and Terri chuckled. "But whenever I returned, there was Maurizio, always a little richer, a little closer to being King Midas, a little more formidable. He studied business, persuaded the banks to lend him money by a process I think must have been akin to hypnotism. He was a terrible risk but they handed over whatever he wanted, anyway." Bruno yelled suddenly, "Hey, Giorgio, what do you mean by giving me an empty bottle, you dog?"

"It wasn't empty when I gave it to you," Giorgio said, grinning as he replaced it.

When he'd drained half the new bottle in a gulp, Bruno continued his story. "Then a man called Torelli, a hotel owner, cheated him on a deal. Maurizio went to him and asked him politely to put the matter right. Torelli laughed in my nephew's face and got his strong-arm men to rough him up. I'll never forget the sight of Maurizio when he staggered home. He was bleeding and covered with bruises, and his eyes were full of a terrible light as he said, 'Let him beware.' Within a year, he'd bankrupted Torelli and bought his hotel at a knock-down price. Today it's the Midas."

Terri gave a slight shudder. "What a frightening story."

"It is," Bruno agreed. "But Maurizio can be a frightening man. He broke Torelli with a cold, single-minded purpose that I still remember in my nightmares. He never forgets a friend who's been good to him, but he never forgives an enemy, and his vengeance is merciless. I take care not to get on his wrong side because I'm a coward. If I were a brave man—" He broke off and shrugged.

"If you were a brave man—what would you do?" Terri asked curiously.

"What's the point of talking about it?" Bruno said with a sigh. "I'm not brave and I'm getting old. I like to sleep soft and know where my next meal's coming from. When I was younger, it was different."

"Bruno, I haven't the faintest idea what you're talking about," Terri said, half laughing, half worried. There was an edge on his voice that puzzled her because it sounded like self-loathing.

"Of course you don't," he said, smiling again. "No matter. Here, take these." He pushed the bag of masks toward her. "I bought them for you."

"For me? That was sweet of you."

"A young woman always needs masks. At your age, you're making the great decisions of your life—who will be your lover, perhaps your husband? Who will father your children? Who can tell who you may need to be while you're making your choice?"

"Thank you. I'm going to enjoy playing with them."

"It's not a game, Teresa. Remember, you won't be the only one in disguise. The other masks are more dangerous for being invisible." He drained his glass and refilled it. "A man pursuing a vendetta always hides his true face," he observed to nobody in particular.

"Bruno," she said, laughing, "you're tipsy."

"So I am. So I am. Well, well."

"In any case, who'd pursue a vendetta against me? I've done nobody any harm."

He regarded her gravely. "I think you've never harmed anyone in your entire life, or ever would. You are generous, gentle and honest, and I pray God that life treats you in such a way that you can stay like that."

"You're *very* tipsy."

"How do you know? How do you know it isn't simply another mask? A tipsy man is forgiven much that would get a sober one a kick in the rear." His manner was so droll that Terri collapsed in laughter. "Let's have something to eat," he said.

"I should be going."

Bruno had leaned back so that his face was half in shadow, and for a moment Terri almost thought he really was wearing a mask. His mouth grinned blandly, but his eyes were no more than dark sockets, revealing nothing. "What's the hurry?" he asked casually. "Are you and Maurizio spending the evening together?"

"No, he's entertaining important business clients."

"Then we can have a little supper. Giorgio, your best pizza and another bottle."

An hour later, replete with pizza and red wine, they strolled out together and through the dark streets toward the Midas. Bruno had an inexhaustible fund of funny stories and he regaled Terri with them until her sides ached. They were laughing together, arms entwined, as they turned the last corner before the Midas. Then their laughter died abruptly.

Maurizio stood there, murder in his eyes.

"Good evening," Bruno sang out.

Maurizio ignored him. His eyes pierced Terri. "Where the devil have you been?" he demanded. He was paler than she'd ever seen him.

"I've been walking home."

"Until this hour? I know how long it takes to walk from the Palazzo Calvani."

"So I took a bit longer," Terri said, getting annoyed at his manner. "So what? I'm not answerable to you for the time I take, am I?"

"I went to meet you and missed you by a few minutes. I came back to wait for you, and when you didn't arrive on time, I thought you'd got lost. I thought of all the things that could have happened to you in the dark byways of this city."

"Nothing happened. I met Bruno, we had a pizza and then walked home."

"How are your business guests?" Bruno asked with a glance at Maurizio's elegant attire. "Surely you're not neglecting them?"

Maurizio threw him a sulphurous glance. "I was about to send out a search party," he said through gritted teeth.

Bruno smiled seraphically. "In that case, my dear boy, it's as well that we arrived before you made yourself look so foolish," he said. "Signorina Teresa, let me thank you for a most charming evening. I'll say good-night now. Don't forget to take these." He handed her the bagful of masks. "You'll need them sooner than you think."

He floated past them into the hotel. Terri tried to follow him but Maurizio stopped her with a hand on her arm. "I don't like being made to look foolish, Teresa," he said quietly.

She was still cross. "In that case, it's a pity you got upset about nothing. Who do you think you are to talk to me like this in a public place, or any place? Now I want to go inside, so kindly get out of my way this minute."

"Are you giving me orders?" Maurizio demanded, his eyes kindling.

"Yes, as a matter of fact, I am."

"And what do you think gives you the right?"

"The fact that I'm paying to stay here," she snapped. "You're the hotelier, I'm a guest in your establishment and I don't like the way you're behaving. In fact, I'll probably make a complaint to the management."

She took advantage of his surprise to slip past him and into the hotel. Maurizio drew a long breath to get his temper under control but he knew he was angry with himself more than her. He'd spent the last few hours in hell, terrified lest something had happened to her. His reason had told him that she was probably exploring, but it was hard to listen to reason when his heart was hammering with dread. The last time he'd felt such overwhelming fear was when Rufio had gone missing, and he'd started the search that had led to his young brother's dead body. And then she'd strolled into view, arm in arm with his roguish uncle, and laughed at him.

With a muttered oath, he went swiftly into the Midas and headed for his office, where Bruno was pouring himself a large brandy. "I thought I'd find you here," Maurizio said grimly.

"And I knew you'd be looking for me, nephew, so I made myself easy to find. But let's be quick. You shouldn't neglect your clients."

"I put my clients off," Maurizio said grimly.

"But I thought a lucrative deal hung on tonight?"

"*It did.*"

"And you risked losing it? My dear boy, welcome to the human race."

Maurizio's eyes glittered. "I'm warning you, don't push me too far. You did this on purpose, didn't you?"

"I bumped into Teresa by accident. . . ."

"And keeping her out so late—was that an accident?"

"You're not her father or her keeper."

"I have reasons for wanting her kept safe—"

"But are they the reasons you think they are?"

"What do you mean?"

"When did you last disappoint business clients?"

"I'm not bandying words about," Maurizio said furiously. "Just tell me—do I have a single secret left?"

"You mean, did I tell her what you're really up to? No, I didn't. I should have, but I didn't. I wasn't brave enough."

Some of the tension went out of Maurizio's face. "That was very wise of you. I strongly advise you to go on not being brave."

He walked out. Bruno poured himself another brandy and regarded it thoughtfully. "But showing you your own heart is another matter, nephew," he murmured. "I'm brave enough for *that*."

* * *

Playing with masks, Terri discovered, was as exciting as being a child opening a present. She tried them on one by one, the silver tinsel one, the black and gold one, the scarlet satin, the white mask with the huge nose.

She returned to the silver half mask with a glittering fringe, and fixed it into place. Suddenly, the door opened and Maurizio came quietly into her room. He approached her without speaking and Terri stayed quite still. His eyes were fixed on the mask. "Columbine," he said in a strange voice. "A cunning minx to tempt a man's soul away. Or just another coquette, teasing him to perdition. Which are you?"

"Which do you think?" she whispered.

"I think you're playing games with me, Teresa—mocking me—and that makes me angry."

"Is it forbidden to mock you, Maurizio?" she asked from behind the safety of the silver tinsel. "Is there a law about it?"

"No, but it's—dangerous."

Suddenly, she knew that there really was something in the old superstition Bruno had told her about. A mask altered the wearer deep down, not merely on the surface. She'd changed into a woman who wasn't afraid of danger, not this kind. "You *terrify* me," she said theatrically.

"That's enough," he said harshly.

"No, it isn't. Not until Columbine says so." She whirled away from him and went to regard her new self in the mirror. A stranger looked back at her, a brilliant, confident stranger who could take this man on, and win. "Bruno was right," she murmured.

Maurizio came up behind her. "What did Bruno say?"

"Oh, lots of things. Very few of them made sense."

"But some of them must have. What did he say, Teresa?"

She shrugged. The tension in Maurizio had communicated itself to her. This controlled man was on the rack and she felt a heady exhilaration in keeping him there. Prim, proper Terri had become a coquette and the pleasure was exquisite.

Maurizio laid his hands on her shoulders and spoke in a quiet voice that held a faint echo of menace. "What did Bruno say?"

"A million things. I can't remember them all."

"But you remember one well enough to think he was right about it. What was Bruno right about?"

"Why does it matter?"

"Teresa, don't do this...."

"Why shouldn't I if I want to?"

He dropped his head and laid his lips against her neck. "Don't do this," he murmured. "Tell me what I want to know."

The excitement of his touch was so fierce that it almost drove everything else from her head. But a small, obstinate part of her refused to relinquish the fun of teasing him. "What do you want to know?" she murmured.

"What did Bruno say?"

She shrugged, laughing at him. "I've forgotten."

"Teresa..."

"Why does it matter, anyway?"

Maurizio knew it was madness to reveal that he was troubled, but he couldn't help himself. She was bewitching, tempting, tormenting, and it was suddenly vital to bring her under his control. "Tell me," he repeated.

"Why, Maurizio?" With a flash of inspiration, she added, "What are you *afraid* he said to me?"

"What do you mean by that?" he asked tensely.

"I think you must have some dark secret. What is it? Won't you tell Columbine?"

"Is that who you are?"

"It's who I am at this moment, but in a few minutes I may be someone else." Quick as a flash, she whirled away from him, snatched off the silver mask and donned another, covered in black sequins and edged with gold. "Who am I now, Maurizio?"

"Someone I don't know," he growled.

"Well, perhaps that's as it should be. Why should you always know who I am? Do you let me know who you are? Right now, for instance. Are you in my room as the proprietor of this hotel, or someone else? What's *your* mask?"

He drew in his breath at how close she'd come to his dangerous secret. "Someone else," he said. "Someone who was concerned for your safety and who's getting precious little thanks for it."

She laughed and it was like the glitter of clear water. "I don't need watching over. I'm perfectly safe."

He had a mad instinct to shout that she wasn't safe at all. She was the victim of a man who was using her to exact revenge, and she should escape him while she could. Then he remembered that he *was* that man, and he rubbed his eyes in total, enraged confusion.

When he lifted his head again, the black mask had been replaced by a half mask of scarlet satin, from behind which she studied him in enchanting mockery. "All right, I'll tell you," she said. "Bruno said it was an old Venetian superstition that a mask didn't just help you pretend to be someone else. It actually made you that person. And he was right.''

"Was he?" Relief made it difficult to speak.

"Well, at this moment I feel I've turned into another woman—one who's got you in a spin." It had to be true, she thought. There was no other way to explain the intoxicating courage that enabled her to provoke this man and enjoy it. "Haven't I, Maurizio?"

He took her by the shoulders. "Do you think I'd admit it if you had?" he demanded thickly.

She laughed up into his face from behind the red satin. "I think you *are* admitting it."

His answer was to pull her against him, looking into her face for a moment before he covered her lips with his own. "Is this what you wanted to know?" he growled against her mouth.

"Yes," she murmured. "This is exactly what I wanted to know."

There was anger and a kind of desperation in his kiss, but they only added to her exhilaration. The scarlet mask was doing its work, making her a woman of shameless appetites, who was willing to reach out to the man she wanted and return his kiss with interest. She wove her fingers through his hair and drew him closer. He trembled as though he was taken aback. But not for long. Suddenly, his tongue was in her mouth, exploring her desperately and wreaking havoc with her senses.

He urged her toward the bed and she went with him naturally. She lay back in his arms, her breathing coming deeper, her breasts rising and falling as he began to open the buttons of her shirt. When he slipped

his hand inside, a long sigh escaped her. It was unbe-
lievably good. His fingers contained magic. They
could set off sparks that flashed all over her body, to
her fingers and toes, to her loins. It felt almost wicked
to experience such pleasure.

The touch of his tongue on her peaked nipple made
another sigh escape her, and she arched instinctively.
No man had ever touched her breasts before. Shame
had always made her fend them off before this point.
But with Maurizio, her shame seemed to vanish, leaving only desire behind. She was possessed by feelings
that were completely new to her, and she wanted more.

He raised his head, leaving his hand there to caress
her subtly. It wasn't enough. She wanted the feeling of
his purposeful tongue, curling around her nipple,
teasing it back and forth, driving her wild with pleasure. "Why have you stopped?" she gasped.

"I wasn't sure it was what you wanted," he murmured.

"Oh yes! Yes, Maurizio. *Yes*—"

He bent his head again and she groaned with
shameless pleasure. She trembled at the physical
delight he could give her and which took her to the
edge of a new world.

He sensed her trembling and his spirits soared. At
last he would discover the secret that had so far eluded
him: the secret of *her*. Then, perhaps, he might have
peace.

"Let me see you without this thing," he growled.
With an impatient movement, he took the mask from
her face and tossed it away. "Now you're you again."

But his words were fatal. Herself was just what Terri
didn't want to be. It was someone else who'd offered
herself up to his lovemaking with shameless aban-

don, and as he forced her to become Terri again, the old shame and reservations came alive. With despair, she felt the magic die, leaving her cold and awkward. "Maurizio..."

"Hush, let me love you..."

"No, wait—please—"

"I've waited so long already." He was kissing her as he spoke, his lips making a determined assault on her face, her neck, her breasts.

"Maurizio, please." She began to struggle. "I can't do this."

She felt him freeze, and when he moved back to look at her, his face was hard. "More games, Teresa?"

"It isn't a game—I swear—I don't know what happened, but I can't...please, I can't!"

He made an angry sound and moved away from her. Terri took a horrified look at her own bare breasts, the peaked nipples telling the unmistakable story of her wantonness, and she hurriedly covered herself. She rose quickly from the bed and turned away from him. "I'm sorry," she said breathlessly.

"Sorry? You play your coquettish tricks on me and say you're *sorry*?"

"It wasn't any trick," she cried angrily. "I couldn't help it. One minute it was all right and the next—it wasn't." She added lamely, "You shouldn't have taken off the mask."

"Are you telling me you can only make love from behind a mask?" he demanded cruelly.

She was pale. "That might just be it."

"Now I've heard everything. Of all the excuses for making a fool of a man—"

"I wasn't trying to make a fool of you." His hard face told her that he didn't believe her. He looked implacable and unforgiving, and she shivered. "Please, Maurizio, I'd like you to go."

"Willingly," he said through clenched teeth. Without a backward look, he strode to the door and slammed it behind him.

Chapter Six

After the way Maurizio had stormed out, Terri wondered if she would ever see him again, but the next night, when once more she left work at nine, he was there waiting for her, leaning against a wall as if he had all evening at his leisure. Her heart leapt, but she kept her manner light as she fell into step beside him. "Does this mean I'm forgiven?" she asked.

"It means I ask *you* to forgive *me*. I overreacted and behaved badly."

"I wasn't playing coquettish games, Maurizio, truly. I just—I don't know what came over me."

"Hush. It's over. I come in sackcloth and ashes."

His expression was so droll that she laughed and relaxed. "Aren't you overreacting again, coming to meet me when you have more important things you should be doing?" she challenged.

"There's nothing more important than taking care of you," he said lightly.

"You speak as if I were in danger."

He shrugged. "All foreigners are in danger in a strange city, especially in winter."

"But Venice isn't strange to me anymore. I've fallen in love with it. I don't believe anything bad could happen to me amid such beauty," she mused, looking around her at the ancient buildings that were half-visible in the gloom.

"Then you haven't studied Venice's history," Maurizio observed. "This has always been a dangerous place, where love and murder walked hand in hand.... Look at that corner," he said, pointing ahead. "Did you see a man slipping away or was it a trick of the light? You can't tell. The shadows promise much but hide everything. And if the man was real, is he lover or assassin? Will he pierce your heart with passion—or a stiletto? When you discover which, it will be too late."

Terri laughed and let him put an arm about her shoulder and draw her close. Maurizio enchanted her when he was in this mood. And then she wondered whether it was the man who enchanted her or the whole mysterious city, of which he was but a part.

"What are you thinking?" he asked quickly, turning her chin up so that he could look into her face.

Caught by surprise, she replied with instinctive honesty, "I was wondering whether it's Venice or you that I—"

"That you what?" he asked when she checked herself.

"That I like so much," she finished lamely.

"Only 'like'? A moment ago, you were in *love* with Venice."

His eyes gleamed at her in the darkness, challenging her with what she'd almost said. Terri shrugged and tried to sound natural. "Like—love—whatever," she said.

"As you say," he answered blandly, but his smile unnerved her.

It was as if he could look into the bottom of her heart and read secrets there that she hadn't even admitted to herself. Even after the disaster of last night, he must know how easily he could evoke her desire. Suddenly, she felt herself blushing from head to toe; every part of her body was burning, out of control. She wanted to touch him and have him touch her, not in the friendly way he was doing now, but intimately, as he'd done the night before. Wanting him was irrational after she'd rejected him, and she was ashamed of her own desire. Her shame at something so natural made her angry with herself, but she couldn't help it.

Abruptly she turned away, freeing herself from Maurizio's arm and heading toward the Midas Hotel with hurrying steps. "Why do you run away from me?" he asked, catching up. "Don't you trust me anymore?"

"I'm not running away from you," she said with a hint of breathlessness. Firmly she slowed her steps, telling herself not to be foolish.

After a moment, his arm went about her shoulder again. "What do you want of me, Teresa? You seem to tell me two different things at once. Do you want me to leave you alone or do you want *this?*"

On the words, he drew her into the shadows. His arms tightened gently about her and the next moment his mouth covered hers. At first he kissed her cautiously, as though anticipating rejection, but Terri was incapable of protest. She'd spent a lonely night, fearing that this joy was lost to her forever. Now her fears were banished. The feel of Maurizio's lips on hers obliterated everything but him, and she was drowning in sensation, fears forgotten, yearning only for this to last forever.

"Teresa," he murmured as he kissed her. "Teresa...tell me that you want me...in spite of everything...."

His burning lips made it impossible for her to answer, nor did she want to answer. She wanted only to stay in his arms until the end of time.

She'd closed her eyes, to enjoy more fully the feeling of being alone in a private world with Maurizio. Now she let them open slightly. Through her lashes she had an eerie sense of seeing all Venice at once. Bridges, palaces, mysterious narrow passages leading to infinity, all seemed to float before her.

And then she tensed at something she thought she'd seen. Opening her eyes wide, she had a glimpse of a man standing on a small bridge nearby. He was immediately below a lamp that threw livid shadows across his face, distorting his features, but she could tell that he was regarding her with an air of puzzlement and sadness. Then he moved, the light on his face changed and at once Terri cried out, *"Leo."*

Maurizio tensed and pushed her away from him, staring intently into her face. "What did you say?" he demanded.

"Leo—my brother—I saw him." She wrenched herself free from Maurizio and ran to the bridge. It was empty. "He was here," she cried. *"I saw him."*

"Or the force of your longing made you imagine him," Maurizio told her.

"I didn't imagine him," she cried fiercely. "He was there and it was Leo."

"Then where is he now?"

"Listen, I can hear footsteps. Over there!" She darted across the bridge and plunged into the maze of passages that confronted her. "Leo," she cried frantically. *"Leo..."*

But there was no sign of him, only the sound of echoing footsteps nearby, then far off. "Leo," she cried again.

"Teresa." Maurizio was by her side, "Stop and think a moment...."

"I've no time to think," she said frantically. "Leo was there. I *saw* him. I must find him."

Before he could stop her, she darted away again, trying to locate the steps, but constantly mocked by their elusiveness. As she ran, the darkened streets were full of echoes, and she couldn't tell which were her own steps and which those of her quarry. She cried his name desperately and the echoes threw it back to her.

At last the chase took her out of the little alleys. She saw a gleam of water and realized she'd come to one of the smaller side canals. Just up ahead, she thought she made out a figure darting over a bridge. She ran faster, trying to catch him, not seeing how close she'd come to the water. There was a shout, a cry of warning. Too late she saw her foot slipping toward the edge of the bank, and the next moment she was falling. She hit the water before she fully understood what was happening, and then there was only the cold darkness engulfing her as she went down, singing in her ears. She thrashed around madly, but there was darkness in all directions, and for a terrible moment she didn't even know which way was up. She had a nightmare vision of sinking forever, condemned to eternal existence in this dreadful void.

Then a hand, apparently from nowhere, seized her firmly. Another hand took hold of her, and she felt herself being pulled up and up, until they broke the surface, and she realized that Maurizio had come in after her and fished her out.

A little way ahead, the stone bank was broken by steps running into the water. He drew her along to them and helped her out. Terri collapsed onto the steps and sat there, coughing and spluttering, shivering from the effect of the chill air on her wet body. Overhead she heard Maurizio yell, "Hey, Pietro," and when she looked up, a gondola was hurriedly approaching. "Get in quickly," Maurizio said. "Pietro, take us to the Midas."

As he spoke, he was almost shoving Terri under the *feltz*. He followed her, pulling curtains tightly closed behind them, and the next moment, the gondola swayed as they cast off. Terri was shivering as much from shock as cold, and Maurizio pulled her into his arms, rubbing her to keep her warm, but also shivering himself. Terri clung to him, taking comfort from the feel of his strong body, and the beat of his heart, which seemed to shake his whole frame.

"Come close to me," Maurizio said urgently. "I'll keep you warm." He tilted her chin so that her face was turned up to him. In the darkness, he couldn't see her face but he could sense her warm breath against his lips. "Teresa," he murmured.

"Did you see him?" she whispered. "Did you see where Leo went?"

He made a soft sound that was perilously like a curse. "Will you forget him?"

"How can I forget him? He's my brother—and something strange has happened to him."

"It wasn't your brother. That's just wishful thinking."

"You don't know that," she insisted.

"Teresa, that was not Leo," he said emphatically. "It couldn't have been."

"Why not? How can you be so sure?"

She sensed a frisson go through him as though the question made him uneasy. "Because—because—why should Leo run away from you?" he said.

"I don't know. That's why I have to find him."

"Teresa, stop this," he said desperately. "You can't spend your life chasing fantasies. You're cold and wet. All that matters now is getting you home before you take a chill."

"I'm not cold," she said, discovering it to be true. Through a crack in the curtains, a light played briefly over Maurizio's face, vanished and appeared again. Terri could just make out his expression turned toward her, intent, angry—and something else that she didn't have time to analyze.

"I'm not cold, either," he said hoarsely. "I'm burning—feel how I burn—*Teresa.*" The last word was muffled as his mouth covered hers again. He held her fiercely, pulling her hard against him.

Terri felt her heart pounding as never before as she surrendered to his kiss. The man she'd glimpsed and lost was forgotten. There was only Maurizio and her growing passion for him, a passion he was doing everything to inflame by the movements of his tongue and the urgent caresses of his hands. He wanted her as much as she wanted him, and the knowledge thrilled her and spurred her on to kiss him back with new ardor. She reached up eager hands and wound her fingers in his hair, offering herself to him completely as his mouth left a trail of burning kisses down the length of her neck. The reserve of years was melting into nothing. In another moment, he would claim her here in the rocking gondola, and she would have no power or will to refuse.

A bump as they touched the landing stage brought her back to herself. "We've arrived," Maurizio said tersely. "Come."

He jumped out, holding Terri's hand to help her up the steps. Before she could go far, he swept her into his arms and ran into the hotel with her, ignoring curious stares from passersby. The lift door was open and he hurried in, not noticing the other occupant until they were on their way up. "Good grief, whatever happened?" Bruno demanded.

"She fell into the water," Maurizio said.

"And you heroically dived in after her?" Bruno asked with raised eyebrows and the suspicion of a wry smile.

"This isn't funny," Maurizio snapped. "I've got to get her dry before she catches pneumonia." His eyes met Bruno's, commanding him to be silent. Bruno's eyebrows lifted again, but he said no more.

As soon as they were in Terri's room, Maurizio set her down and began to strip off her sodden clothes. "Get the rest of your things off quickly," he growled, tossing her dress aside.

"What about you? You could catch cold, too."

He gave an unexpected smile that seemed to flow right through her. "I'm Venetian," he said softly.

"The water of my city is as natural to me as dry land. It's strangers who have to take care." Abruptly he left her, heading for the bathroom. Terri realized that she was almost naked. Her underwear clung to her revealingly, and she was swept by a wave of self-consciousness. Maurizio returned with a towel and a bathrobe, which he tossed to her. Then he returned to the bathroom and shut the door.

Terri hurriedly threw off her underclothes and wrapped herself in the bathrobe, which belonged to the Midas and was the color of gold. It was too large and enveloped her chilled body gloriously. She rubbed her hair until it was almost dry, then sat down at the dressing table to comb it out. The woman who looked back at her from the mirror was a mass of confusion, with everything reflected in her face. There was the brief joy of thinking she'd found Leo, the anguish of seeing her hope destroyed, but most of all there was the memory of Maurizio's embrace. The feel of his arms about her was still there and his kiss seemed to be imprinted on her lips.

She drew a long breath as it all came back to her, and she closed her eyes, feeling heat stream through her body. She was as conscious of him as if he were crushing her against him, caressing her lips with his own. Now that she was alone, she could admit the truth to herself, and the truth was that she wanted him with all the passion of which she was capable, passion that had been stifled for too long. For years, her barriers had been in place, but now this man had swept them aside, releasing something deep within her that threatened to consume her. The fears of last night were gone, and she was eager to yield to her desire. She could no longer hide that from herself.

She opened her eyes and caught her breath at what she saw. Maurizio had come silently out of the bathroom and was standing watching her. He, too, had changed into a bathrobe, which was roped in lightly at the waist in such a way that the top hung open, revealing his brown, muscular chest. He moved slowly toward her, his eyes meeting hers in the mirror, until he was standing immediately behind her. Only then did Terri realize that her own robe had fallen wide open, revealing her breasts, with the peaked nipples that told the story of her desire. For a brief moment, the old shyness returned and she made an instinctive movement to cover herself, but before she could succeed, Maurizio had dropped his head to lay his lips against her cheek. Their touch was light but it was as if he'd burned her with coals. Searing awareness went through her and she threw her head back, offering herself to him ecstatically. She could feel his fingers at the edge of the robe, pulling it back and down her arms.

He ran his hands hungrily over her while his lips moved softly over her jaw to her throat. Terri reached up to weave her fingers through his hair, breathing deeply as waves of pleasure flowed through her, turning her eager body to pure fire.

Maurizio felt himself torn. Every fiber of his being wanted what was happening now, wanted to touch and caress her, to bury himself in her, to revel in the warmth of her, wanted *her*. And now she was here, her beautiful, almost naked body ready for him, and there was nothing to hold him back. Nothing except the gambler's caution, an instinct for calculating all the odds before he made his move. That instinct was too deep-rooted to be easily defeated, but now it was almost drowned by the clamor of his senses. Her skin was smooth beneath his hands, her lips were honey against his and the scent of heat and eager expectation were almost driving him mad. Caution was becoming lost in a wild desire for possession at all costs.

Of course, Elena's daughter was a temptress, skilled in inflaming a man, rejecting him once, only to set a higher value on herself. But before the thought was complete, it was swept away by the knowledge that this had nothing to do with his revenge. At this moment, she wasn't Elena's daughter. She was *Teresa,* and Teresa was everything that was beautiful and desirable in a woman. He was caught up in a whirlwind of desire. She *had* to be his. There could be no other way for this to end.

He twisted his body and sat down beside her, his back to the mirror, and pulled her across him so that she lay in his arms, her head cradled against his shoulder. He brushed his fingers against one peaked nipple and felt her whole body tremble. Then she was still, but it wasn't a passive stillness. The breath coming through her slightly parted lips was ragged and her eyes were fixed intently on his, speaking to his senses in a silent language. It would be so easy now to carry her to the bed and take the rich feast that was offered him—too easy. "If you want me to leave, you must say so now," he said hoarsely. "After this, there's no turning back." He bent low to whisper against her lips, "Answer me."

She took a long time to answer, as though the decision racked her, and for a dreadful moment he feared that the treasure was to be snatched from him again. But at last he heard and felt her reply breathed softly against his mouth. "I want you to stay, Maurizio."

"You must be very sure, Teresa."

"I'm sure, I'm—sure—" The last word was lost in the stampede of her senses. She felt as though a spell had been cast over her, destroying the will to do anything else but this. She knew that what was happening now was only the completion of something that had started the moment they'd met. She'd looked into Maurizio's eyes and wanted him with a fierce, sensual longing that she'd never dared recognize until this moment. But now the die was cast. She could do nothing but yield to the clamorous demands of her body that said only he could satisfy her.

"Maurizio," she whispered, and felt his arms tighten about her.

"Say that you want me," he said in a voice that was half demand, half plea.

"I want you." The words were wrenched from her depths.

He rose, drawing her to her feet also, and pulled off his robe. Hers followed, and he took her in his arms. The feeling of her nakedness pressed against his gave her a moment of awkwardness, but it quickly passed. Maurizio was touching her body everywhere, giving subtle caresses that passed quickly but left a trail of ecstasy behind them. Soon she could think of nothing but where he might touch her next, where she urgently wanted him to touch her next. Tentatively she reached for him and was entranced by the sensation of his smooth skin against her fingers. She'd never explored a man's body before, but the intense feelings he evoked in her made her crave to do just that. He was *Maurizio,* and therefore different from all other men.

His body was an instant delight, warm and smooth with hard muscles that she could feel beneath the skin.

Again she had the overwhelming awareness of the barely leashed power in his frame, the same awareness that she'd recognized at their very first meeting, and which, she now realized, had physically excited her even then. Her life had been quiet and she'd been content to have it so, believing that this was her nature. But the only man to make her senses sing was a man of danger, and it thrilled her.

He drew her onto the bed and lay beside her. He kissed her face, her neck, her breasts, cupping their fullness in his hands while his lips teased the nipples. Nothing in her life had ever felt like that, so good, so sweet. Her body seemed to have developed a life of its own. It responded to his kisses and caresses by arching against him, while blind instinct made her wind her fingers in his hair and draw his face more completely against her breasts. The slow, powerful beating of her heart felt like the rhythm of the whole world, urging her on.

Maurizio drew back a little to look down at her and she had a glimpse of his manhood, hard and powerful, ready for her as she was ready for him. All the excitement coursing through her body seemed to be directed to the one, throbbing place between her legs, where she wanted him.

He whispered her name softly. Through the clamor of passion, Terri detected a strange note in his voice, as though he were troubled. "Maurizio," she whispered.

For a brief instant, Madge was there in her mind, crying out her life-denying accusation with all its spite and bitterness. But the next moment, Madge was gone, swept away by the tide of passion. She knew now that she was right to yield to her desire, because something so deliriously sweet and wonderful could only be a gift from the gods. It couldn't be wrong to love a man with such fierce intensity that nothing mattered but to meld her being with his.

She could feel the moment of that blazing union approaching and her soul was joyful as she went to meet her destiny. As he moved over her, it felt right and natural to part her legs in welcome. The moment of his entry was a piercing, unfamiliar shock, then all sense of strangeness vanished. He was there, inside her, where she wanted him. She began to move her hips, trying to feel him more profoundly, wanting to weep with joy. It was an ecstatic sensation that made a pale mockery of all other sensations in her life. The Venetians were right; only love mattered. Only *this* mattered, this blissful union with the beloved, this perfect meeting of flesh and flesh, bringing together two halves of a whole.

His face was there above her, dark, concerned. "Are you all right?"

"Yes," she whispered. "Oh, yes."

"Are you sure? I didn't know—I never dreamed—"

She had no idea what he meant. She was lost in a delirious dream of desire in which there was only sensation and emotion, and the perfect fusion of the two.

"Maurizio." She murmured his name in a plea for she knew not what. But she understood that this had to continue to its appointed end, and that end must be glorious. He was thrusting into her slowly, making her wild with pleasure and the tormenting realization that he was holding something back. *"Maurizio..."*

He was kissing her face. "Yes? Tell me," he murmured.

"I want you. I want—everything."

He drove into her again, more deeply but with a controlled power that made her gasp. "Are you all right?" he asked again.

"Yes—yes—go on."

The rhythm possessed her body, her mind, her consciousness. There was nothing in the world but this driving, exquisite repetition of pleasure. With each thrust she was carried to a new peak of delirious joy. A loud cry broke from her and she drew him close against her, thrusting back at him with her hips, trying to capture the feeling and hold it fast forever. But it was fruitless. As she felt herself carried to the pinnacle, she knew that the depths yawned beneath them. But not yet—not yet—

Despite the buildup, the final moment took her by surprise, catching her and tossing her helplessly into the storm. Before she knew it, she was being spun around and thrown upward to glorious, unimaginable heights. Pleasure pervaded her body and she gave herself up to it with abandon until the final explosion of sensation had left her drained, exhausted and happy.

She lay catching her breath, so overwhelmed by what had happened that she was momentarily speechless. But when she turned happily to Maurizio, she was shocked to see him looking distraught.

"Maurizio, what—?"

He sat up and turned to look at her. "I didn't know," he said. "Oh, God, I never thought—but I should have known—it was staring me in the face all the time."

"Didn't know what?" Terri asked.

"That you were a virgin," he said with a groan.

"Why, what difference can it possibly make?" she asked, puzzled.

He looked into her shining eyes, and looked away again quickly. Her unreserved honesty pierced him like an accusation. She was genuine through and through. The two-faced temptress had been a figment of his imagination.

Terri propped herself on her elbow to look him in the eye. "Do you mean I turned out to be a disappointment?" she asked. But there was no apprehension in her eyes. Already she had the look of a woman who knew her own power.

A memory of her warmth and sweetness melting against him scorched his mind. "No," he said with tender irony. "You weren't a disappointment. One day—it might be the other way around."

"One day?" she asked gaily. "Who cares about one day? I don't even care about the next hour. I'm happy now. Suddenly, nothing seems to matter but this." She pushed him back against the pillows and threw herself across his chest in delicious abandon. "I'm so glad it happened," she said passionately.

Maurizio was relieved that Terri couldn't see his face. Despite his skill at keeping it expressionless, he knew that it would reveal everything now—his guilt, his torment, above all the secret he was keeping from her, and which suddenly seemed so monstrous.

He tried to think practically but his brain seemed to have seized up. He knew he should go away from her right now and not come near her until he'd sorted out a hideous situation that she knew nothing about. But as he lay there telling himself what he ought to do, he was becoming increasingly aware of her breasts against his chest. There was a sense of inevitability about the way his arms settled around her, and a heart-stopping beauty about her face, coming alight with eager anticipation.

"Maurizio," she whispered.

He had a last moment of sanity when his conscience shouted that he mustn't do this—not until she knew the wrong he'd done her, and forgiven him. But conscience counted for nothing against the roaring of his senses and the delight that flooded through his heart and his body at the thought of loving her again. She laid her lips against his, kissing him with an urgent sense of purpose. It was the kiss of a woman who'd finally discovered her own passionate sexuality, who knew what she wanted and was determined to have it. With an equal mixture of dismay and joy, Maurizio recognized that there was no way to resist her.

He began to kiss her, caressing her face, her breasts, her curved hips. Her slight, delicate body looked tiny beside his great frame, yet she had a magic that canceled out his strength.

Terri received his lovemaking as a kind of glory. Now she knew him and herself. A long road had opened up before her, leading to infinite delight, and she was eager to travel it with him. The memory of their first loving was still in her flesh, making it respond even more readily. His lips on her breasts sent fires thrilling through her. She gave a long sigh of blissful anticipation and at once he looked up, smiling at her with tender eyes.

There had been many women in Maurizio's life, yet he had the unnerving sensation that this was the first time he'd ever made love. Her every movement, every response was a revelation. At their first meeting, she'd made him think of spring and he'd brushed the thought aside, feeling his heart encased in winter. Now he discovered that spring could banish winter, making young shoots burst from the snow, filling the world with new life. Everything else vanished. All the troubling circumstances that would complicate their love counted for nothing. Between them they'd created a cocoon in which only they could live, and for a few precious minutes it protected them.

When he parted her legs, she moved quickly to draw him over her, eager to have him inside her and know the joy of complete union again. Despite the passion raging through him, entering her was like coming home to peace. But there was no time to wonder about the contradiction, for he was lost in the rhythm, driven on by a desire to possess her and share in the magic quality that made her special. She cried out his name and clung to him. Together they reached the burning heights, and for one brief moment his hopes were realized. She was his, part of him, letting him be part of her.

But when the separation came, he was himself again, black with deception against her shining honesty, and he discovered with bitterness that there was no escape from his own being. He lay holding her while his heart slowed its beating and his mind went on its old tortured way. Perhaps now was the moment to tell her everything. If he confessed while she was still soft with the tenderness of their loving, might she not forgive him?

But while he was trying to pluck up the courage to speak, he heard a small sound from her, and looked down to find her asleep against his chest, a contented smile on her face.

Chapter Seven

In the early morning, Maurizio left Terri's room, moving like a sleepwalker, stunned by what had happened to him. In a few devastating hours, his world had been turned upside down. The glow from Terri's trusting eyes had bathed his inner landscape in a new light. Everything he'd believed was true turned out to be folly. His own actions, so justifiable when he'd planned them, now looked unforgivable in the light of her innocence, the one thing he hadn't calculated on.

Guilt lay on him like a black weight, not only over his plan to use her to gain revenge on Elena Calvani, but because of something worse. Something so much worse that the thought of it was enough to make him groan.

As he approached his room, he heard footsteps behind him and turned to see Bruno running up the stairs as lightly as a young man. He was smiling sheepishly.

"I know, I know," he said. "I ought to be ashamed of myself at my age. I am, I promise you. But when a lady is willing, what can a man do?" He checked himself and stared at Maurizio. "My God, you look terrible!"

Dazed, Maurizio didn't answer. Bruno took his arm and urged him the rest of the way to Maurizio's room. When the door had closed behind them, he said, "What's happened? Has she discovered the worst about you?"

"Not yet," Maurizio said. "But she soon will."

Bruno looked at him closely. "And that matters?"

"Yes," Maurizio said heavily. "It matters."

Bruno shrugged. "My dear boy, why? After all, what is she but a pawn in your game of revenge? Does a pawn have opinions? Does a man care about them?"

"You know better than that," Maurizio said harshly. He couldn't bring himself to discuss the night he'd spent with Terri, but the urge to confess at least some part of the situation to this wise, kindly man was strong.

"Well, it's about time you found someone whose opinion you care about," Bruno observed. "My felicitations. You'll get off more lightly than you deserve. All you need do is forget about revenge. She need never know that you started your relationship in a state of—shall we say—less than total honesty? It's how a relationship ends that matters. Love her as she deserves to be loved and I won't betray your secret."

Maurizio turned burning eyes on him. "You don't understand," he said. "There's more."

Bruno reached into the drinks cupboard and poured himself a brandy. "Evidently I'm going to need this," he said. "What more can there be?"

Maurizio's hands were balled so tightly that the knuckles turned white. "I know where her brother is," he said quietly.

"You mean you've traced him? What's so terrible about that? She'll fall into your arms with gratitude."

"You don't understand. I've *always* known where he was."

Bruno drank a large mouthful and stared at his nephew, aghast. "Are you saying that *you* spirited him away?"

"No. I took him to my olive estate for a visit. He became very ill. He's been there ever since. The fever left his mind confused."

"Dear God!" Bruno breathed. He stared at Maurizio, meeting his eyes directly.

"Don't say it," Maurizio snapped. "Just don't say it."

"I wouldn't dream of saying anything. Nothing I could say would be equal to this situation." Bruno drained his glass abruptly. "I'm going to my room, and I'm going to stay there. I don't want to bump into Teresa. I can't tell her the truth and I can't look into her eyes and not tell her, so I'm going to be a coward and hide. As for what you're going to do—I just can't imagine." He got out of the room quickly.

Maurizio poured himself a drink and stared out of the window, trying to organize his disordered thoughts. He was suddenly more frightened than ever before in his life. He had to find a way of confessing to Terri that he'd known her brother's whereabouts all along, and somehow he must do it without alienating her—if that were possible. He shuddered as he thought of all the things she could justifiably say to him, of how she might hate him, and how that hate could smother the miracle that had started to happen between them.

But it wasn't in his nature to anticipate defeat. His way was to plan, to scheme, to find methods to avert disaster. Already his subtle brain was working, devising a method to blunt her anger by restoring her brother to her.

Yes, that was it. He would reunite her with Leo, and in the joy of that reunion, she would forgive Maurizio the wrong he'd done her. The situation wasn't irretrievable. His gamblers' instincts were working again, reassuring him that there was a path out of his difficulties. It was going to be hard, but he would manage—somehow....

He lay down and slept uneasily for an hour and awoke still troubled. For once, the revelation of a way out hadn't entirely cleared his mind. His inner eye could see Terri looking at him in disillusion, and he flinched before her horrified gaze. He showered, seeking absolution in the cold water, but she was still there, still looking at him—not shocked now, but sad, saying goodbye.

His mood of self-castigation was so unusual that he became irritable. When he did his morning rounds of the kitchen, the staff took one look at his expression and kept their heads down. Those unfortunate enough to incur his displeasure were sent scuttling.

But then he went into the restaurant where breakfast was being served, and the first thing he saw was Terri sitting at a table by the window, watching for him. When he appeared, her face lit up. It was a frank revelation of joy with nothing held back, so different from a hundred women he'd known who rationed their feelings to get a man where they wanted him. He wondered how he could ever have thought Terri was a coquette.

Her smile had a magical effect, making his temper vanish and laying a balm on his heart. He went to her at once and sat down facing her across the table. When she reached out her hand, he took it, holding it between both of his. He wanted to say something but suddenly there was no need for words. It was enough to sit here, looking into her eyes and feeling the warmth of her happiness radiating out to encompass him. He hadn't known that such feelings could exist. Until last night, his cold heart had protected him, but now there was nowhere left to hide.

"It's such a long time since you went away," she said softly.

"Yes." He couldn't think of anything else to say. He just wanted to sit here, reveling in her beauty and innocence.

"I nearly called your room to say—"

"To say what?" he asked tenderly.

"To say 'come back,' I suppose."

"I wish you had," he said, meaning it. He wanted to look away from Terri. Her heart was in her eyes and he was riven by guilt at the chasm between what he was and what she thought of him.

"Am I going to see you today?" she asked. "Or will you be too busy?"

"Don't you have to work?"

"I could take the day off. Elena won't mind."

He wasn't strong enough to resist. "Then we'll spend today together. We'll take a boat and go to Murano. It's quiet there and we can be away from the crowds." When they were alone together, he promised himself, he would confess everything.

"That would be nice," she said.

She joined him at the landing stage a few minutes later and he swung the motorboat right, along the Grand Canal, then right again, along the Canale della Misericordia that cut through a large section of the city, to bring them out into the lagoon. Almost immediately, Terri saw a small island surrounded by a wall, over the top of which she could just make out pine trees. "Is that Murano?"

"No, that's San Michele, the Venetian cemetery," he answered. "Murano is just beyond. It's a group of islands, like a mini-Venice, but not glamorous like the main city. The people who live there are mostly poor."

At last Murano came in sight, a collection of canals and bridges. As Maurizio had said, it had none of the glitter of the place they'd just left, but it looked natural and lived-in, and Terri liked it at once.

Maurizio tied up at a landing stage on the outskirts of Murano and gave her his hand as she climbed the steps. "Do you have friends that live here?" she asked.

"I did have, once, because this is where I spent my childhood. But I'm afraid I've lost touch with them."

"You lived here? Where?"

"Just here," he said, leading her to a small, shabby house overlooking the lagoon. "My parents rented it. Now it's mine. I use it as a place of escape."

"So you're not just King Midas, after all?" she said, laughing. "Or have you gold plated everything inside?"

"Wait and see." He unlocked the front door and showed her in. Terri looked around curiously at the tiny house with its terrazzo floors, painted walls and odd bits of plain furniture. There were a couple of cheap pictures but otherwise no ornaments. It was almost impossible to imagine the elegant, authoritative Maurizio ever living here. "I expect you're wondering why I kept it?" he said, watching her face.

"Something like that."

"Maybe to remind myself *not* to become King Midas."

Terri noticed something scratched into the stonework over the door. Peering at it, she could just make out the words *Ca' d'oro.* "House of gold," she said. "It must have been you who wrote that."

"No, that was my mother, a week after her marriage. She was very happy in those days, so she often told me. And when I was a child, I remember her singing as she worked. Her happiness made this a real house of gold. She told me that only love built a house of gold, and that I would find a different treasure in every room." He was silent a moment, touching the words with his fingertips. "She loved my father deeply," he said softly. "But then he died, soon after Rufio was born. She was never the same again." He seemed to come out of a reverie. "The house is dear to me because here I have the clearest memories of her."

"What was she like?" Terri asked eagerly.

He considered. "She wasn't beautiful—at least, she was once before grief and toil wore her down. But when her physical beauty faded, there was another beauty that nothing could erase. She was simple and good. You could read her heart in her eyes and what you saw was always true and honest. She was incapable of a mean or petty thought, incapable of cruelty, of deviousness—" He stopped. Terri's clear eyes were fixed on him and the sight smote him. Guilt lashed him, and with it came fear.

"What is it?" she asked.

"Nothing, I just . . . realized how much like her you are. Let me show you around."

Downstairs, there was only the kitchen and one living room. Unlike the rest, the kitchen had been modernized. It looked as though Maurizio really did spend some time here, if the gleaming new coffeepot was anything to go by. Her curiosity about him increased.

He took her hand and led her upstairs, which consisted of two bedrooms and a bathroom, all cramped. He pushed open a door to the smaller bedroom. "This was my room," he said.

"And when you stay here, you still sleep in this room," Terri said, glancing at the bed which was made up.

"Yes. When I was a boy, I used to sit at this window and watch the sun come up over Venice. The city is too far away to see clearly, but that only added to the magic. There was always a certain point when the domes of St. Mark's were touched with gold. I could just make out the glow, and I used to imagine that the whole city was like that. I promised myself that one day I'd find the gold and make it mine. Since then—" he drew her gently into his arms "—I've discovered that there are so many different kinds of gold. A man can pursue it single-mindedly and throw away everything that matters. Or he can recognize the gold that he holds in his arms, and treasure it—and keep it."

His mouth touched hers on the final words. She pressed herself eagerly against him and gave herself up to his kiss. She'd been waiting for this moment ever since he'd left her bed last night, anticipating it eagerly. But no anticipation could subdue the first shock of joy that his lips gave her. The feel of his hard body against hers was doubly exciting now. Last night they'd crossed a boundary and today the world was changed. In his arms she'd found joyful surrender and passionate triumph, sweet tenderness and utter fulfillment, and she would never be whole until she could know those feelings again.

She moved her lips against his, consciously inciting him, and had the pleasure of sensing the uncontrollable response his body communicated. She was ready for the moment when his tongue entered her mouth, exploring her with subtle movements that triggered shivers of pleasure through her. She touched his face, then slid her hands into his hair, relishing the feeling of the springy black locks.

Maurizio drew back a little and spoke in a shaking voice. "We ought to stop this now."

"Why?" she murmured against his lips.

"It's my fault for touching you at all—I shouldn't have—"

"Isn't it a little late to say that?" she whispered, stroking his face with her fingertips.

"I know I sound crazy," he said in a strained voice that showed she was having her effect. "But you're so vulnerable—we should talk before—I mean, there are things—Teresa, will you stop doing that a moment?"

"Don't you like it?"

"I like it."

"Is all this a way of saying you don't want me?"

"No, it isn't."

"Then I guess I'll just keep on doing what I'm doing."

Desperately he seized her hand. "Will you listen to me?" he groaned. "All my life—if I wanted something, I just took it. I never questioned my right to do that."

"And you feel you did that with me?"

"Didn't I?"

"No, dammit! It was my decision, too, even if you don't think so. What is it, Maurizio? Why do you hesitate?" When he didn't answer, she asked, "You're not still worried because I was a virgin?"

"Let's say—it troubled me that you were so different from what I'd imagined. It was like going to bed with one person and awakening with another."

She laughed gaily and snuggled against him in a way that made his heart sing. "The answer's simple," she said.

"What?"

"Let's go back to bed and get better acquainted. Come on." She took his hand.

"Teresa, are you sure you know what you're doing?"

"After last night?" she asked with a touch of hilarity. "Yes, I think I know what I'm doing. And I want to do it."

Still he hesitated. Terri regarded him lovingly, touched by his concern for her. But concern wasn't what she needed right now. She released his hand, moved a little way off and stood where he could see her. She was wearing slacks and a shirt, which she proceeded to open, button by button, before his fascinated gaze. He held his breath. If only everything could be made right between them, what loving they could have.

Terri finished the last button and tossed the shirt away. She wore no bra and her bare breasts had a pearly beauty that made something catch in his throat. The dark areolas about her nipples were an enticement, reminding him of the night before and the joy that had been his. His loins thrilled with the memory and he felt his fragile control slipping away.

Terri came to stand before him and started to work on his buttons, too. "If you're going to be such a blushing violet, I'll have to do something decisive," she said.

"Nobody's ever called me a blushing violet yet," he said huskily.

"Then why am I having to do all the work?" she said, chuckling. "I want you, Maurizio, and I'm going to have you." She was working on the fastening of his slacks. "Do you object?"

"No," he said tightly. "I don't object."

He didn't wait for her to finish, but ripped off the rest of his clothes. She was there ahead of him, jumping onto the bed in delightful nakedness and opening her arms to him. "Come to me," she said, and he went eagerly.

As he made love to her, he gave thanks for her. She was spring and summer rolled into one. Her discovery of passion had enriched her. Now she enriched him in return, giving him all of her self, with nothing held back. The full-hearted generosity of that gift overwhelmed him. She offered up her body to his touch, his kisses, and at the same time she reveled in him. In the few hours since their last loving, she'd gained the confidence to put him off while she explored him, running delicate fingers down his chest and across his flat stomach. When he tried to move, she pushed him back on the bed so that she could lean back and survey him.

"You're blushing," she challenged him hilariously.

To his annoyance he could feel his face going red. "I'm just not used to—this—" Self-consciously, he indicated her critical appraisal of him. "Why don't we—"

"No, why don't we just go on doing what we're doing?" she said firmly, pushing him back. "I prefer it this way." She let her fingers caress his proud manhood and watched the reaction on his face. "Don't you like me doing that, Maurizio?" she asked innocently.

"It's—hard to say," he said raggedly.

"No, it isn't. It's easy. I think you like it. It offends your sense of propriety, but you still *like* it, don't you?"

"*Yes.*"

He was hard and straight in her hand and she surveyed him with frank delight, taking a mischievous pleasure in his discomfiture. She didn't need to ask why her control so disconcerted him. This man was used to appraising, not being appraised, but she wasn't going to let him put her off.

"Well?" he demanded with an edge on his voice. "Do you approve?"

She tilted her head to one side. "I'm not sure. Let's put him to the test."

One second before he exploded, he caught the gleam of mischief in her eyes and his temper died. The next moment, he was caught up in her laughter and they were enfolded in each other's arms, rocking back and forth in joyful mirth. At some point in this paroxysm, he exerted his greater strength to get her onto her back. "Now," he said firmly, "let's do this the traditional way from now on."

"Yes, let's," she said happily. "I give in, I give in."

But despite her words, they both knew that in an important sense it was he who had yielded. What followed was heart stopping in its passion and fulfillment, but also in its gaiety. And Maurizio, who had never associated sex with laughter in his life, found himself dazzled, astonished, enchanted—and more than ever, fearful of the future.

They dozed for an hour. Terri opened her eyes to find Maurizio looking down on her tenderly. "Who was wrong?" he asked.

"I beg your pardon?"

"You were muttering in your sleep. You kept saying, 'You were wrong...you were wrong all the time.' Who was wrong—and about what?"

"Madge," she said. "She was my mother—at least, I thought so for a long time. When I was fifteen, I discovered she wasn't. My father was really my father but he fell in love with—someone else. When she had Leo and me, he adopted us. Madge guessed the truth and told me everything after he died. She said my mother was a slut. The first time she caught me kissing a boy, she made me feel like a slut, as well. I suppose I went on believing it."

She wondered if he would ask her about her real mother's identity, but he didn't and she pushed it aside for later. Just now she was taking frank enjoyment in the sight of his naked body and uncompromising maleness. She reached up and touched his throat with the tip of one finger, letting it trail sensuously down his chest.

"Was that why—" he seemed to be speaking with an effort "—there was no other man before me?" He seized her hand, removed it from his body, where it was wreaking havoc, and kissed the tips of her fingers.

"Yes, that was why. I could never relax with any man. Madge was always there in my head, calling me a slut, telling me I'd turn out no better than my mother, who'd borne two illegitimate children to a married man. I felt crushed by it, and I could never bring myself to trust a man." She stopped for a moment and looked intently at his face. "Why, Maurizio, what's the matter?"

"Nothing," he said hastily.

"You suddenly had a terrible look on your face. Not exactly a frown—it was more as if—I don't know—"

"There's nothing wrong. You imagined it," he insisted. It would have been impossible to tell her that she'd just added to his burden of guilt.

"I used to hate her for putting that voice in my head that I couldn't get rid of," Terri said seriously. "I was afraid it would be there all my life, making me frozen and incapable of ever being close to a man. But I don't hate her anymore. *You* drove her away." She lay back and looked up at him with an innocent sensuality that smote his heart. He still had hold of her hand but she'd brought the other hand into play, tracing lines on his chest again in a way that made his breath come raggedly. "I know now that she was wrong. It doesn't make me a slut to want you as much as I do," she whispered.

"What does it make you?" he couldn't resist asking.

She laughed suddenly. *"Greedy,"* she cried, and pounced without warning, tickling him with feverish speed. He fended her off, also laughing, but she returned to the attack, caressing and kissing his body with devouring intensity. The awkward, unaware young woman of only a day ago had become a pagan nymph, sensual, erotic, at ease with her own body. Tenderness fled, taking subtlety with it. Now her young, newly awakened body demanded sexual fulfillment for its own sake, and she came on to him with astonishing force, claiming her own needs without asking what suited him. If he hadn't been so riven with guilt, he'd have been delighted by this new side of her. As it was, her laughing face and frank lust granted him a glimpse of a glorious world from which he was excluded by his own actions.

"Love me, Maurizio—love me," she coaxed. "Love me everywhere—every way—inside me—" As she spoke, she was urging him, parting her legs in irresistible invitation. No power on earth could have held him back then. As he became one with her, it felt like coming home.

"Yes," she breathed, "like that—like that—I want you, Maurizio, I want you."

She was demanding, coaxing, imperious, playful, and his heart melted. His loins and thighs were like steel and he put all his skill at her service, thrusting slowly, drawing the moment out and watching her flushed face with delight.

"Please," she murmured at last, "please—*now*—"

"Wait," he teased.

She was gasping. "No—*now*—" She arched against him, driving him on and overcoming his will with her own. A cry broke from her as her moment came, and while he was reveling in her climax, he was overtaken by his own, exploding with such profound pleasure that it left him drained and gasping.

When they'd both recovered, he drew her close. "I can't believe that I found you," he said, touching her face gently. "You're perfect, sweet and good and gentle."

"I've got a temper," she said darkly.

"I don't believe it. I'd trust my life to your honesty, to your goodness of heart. What other virtues do you have, I wonder?"

The joy that was bubbling up inside Terri was like a kind of madness. "Why, all of them, of course," she said recklessly. "At least, you're supposed to believe that."

"And I do believe it. I believe that you can be all things, kind and loving—perhaps you can also be forgiving."

"Will I need to be forgiving?" she teased him.

He hesitated before saying slowly, "When two people dare to come very close to each other, they always discover things that need forgiveness."

She frowned, puzzled by something uneasy in his tone. "What do you think you'll have to forgive me?"

"Nothing," he said quickly. "Nothing at all, for you are perfect."

"And so are you."

"No," he said seriously. "I've lived a hard life. What I have, I've gained by fighting and clawing, sometimes by being ruthless. I've had to trust my own judgment, and occasionally my judgment—that is— no man is infallible—"

"Maurizio, what are you talking about? Do you think I care about your business decisions? The only thing that matters to me is what's in your heart—" she touched him over the heart "—the man you truly are in there. Don't you understand?"

For answer, he took her hand and laid his lips against the palm, making her soul sing with joy. "I dare say you've had to be—well, unscrupulous," she said. "Maybe I should care about that but I don't, I can't. I only care that you're true to me and I know that you are."

His face lightened. "You do? Tell me how you know that, Teresa."

"I feel it when you hold me in your arms. I can tell from the beat of your heart against mine, and the feel of your lips when you kiss me. But most of all, I can see it in your eyes." She took his face between her hands and looked deep into his eyes. "I can look into the bottom of your heart," she said softly, "and what I see there fills me with happiness. Whatever you are to anyone else, I know that you're good and true to me."

"My God!" Maurizio said hoarsely. "Oh, my God!"

"Now tell me," she said gently. "What can I possibly have to forgive you for?"

To her surprise, a violent tremor went through him, and when he smiled it seemed to be with effort. "I have to go away and leave you," he said. "We've only just found each other, but I have to go at once. Will you forgive me for that?"

"Of course, as long as you promise to come back to me. Are you going far, or for long?"

"I'm going to an olive estate I have near Rome—"

"Can't I come with you?"

"One day you will, but not now. I have a lot of estate business to see to at Terranotte and you'd find it very boring."

"I wouldn't be bored if I was with you," she said eagerly.

"I'll take you to Terranotte, but not this time."

She had an odd sense of a blank wall behind his smile, but she was too deeply in love to notice danger signals. "I shall begin to think you've got a dark secret there, like Mr. Rochester," she chuckled.

"Like who?"

"He was the hero in *Jane Eyre,* a famous English novel. He had a mad wife that he kept hidden away from the world, and tried to marry the heroine. *She* really had something to forgive."

"I promise you that I have no wife, mad or otherwise, hidden at Terranotte."

"But you've got *something* hidden there," she teased. "Something you don't want me to find out about—"

"I didn't say—" He checked himself uneasily. A gleam of mischief came into her eyes, making her enchanting but deepening his apprehension. She was walking over a snake pit but she didn't see it.

"Let's see—" She scratched her head and pretended to think hard. "You've got a harem?"

"No harem, I swear."

"A dead body, then." She chuckled. "That's it. You've committed a murder and the body's buried in the olive grove and—"

"It's nothing like that," Maurizio said quickly. "This is all your imagination." His smile had faded and his voice was suddenly strained. "You blew it up out of nothing. Let's drop this subject. I'll be back in a couple of days."

Suddenly, there seemed to be a chill in the air. Terri chided herself for taking the joke too far and irritating him. That was all it was, she assured herself.

They returned to Venice in the early light. Maurizio saw her to her room, kissed her goodbye and went to throw some clothes into a bag, for his trip south. As he entered his room, his heart was high with hope. With luck, by this time next day he would have restored Leo to his sister.

The first thing he saw was a light winking on his telephone, signaling that there was a message. He dialed the switchboard and grunted, "Yes?"

"Rinaldo Passi has called you from Terranotte ten times in the last twenty-four hours," the operator informed him. "He said it was urgent but nobody knew how to contact you."

A cold hand clutched Maurizio's stomach. Quickly he dialed the number of Terranotte and in a few moments was talking to his estate manager. "What is it?" he barked.

"*Signore,* something terrible has happened. Signor Leo is missing."

"What the devil—you mean he's got lost somewhere on the estate?"

"Missing. Gone. Completely vanished. He went for a stroll and when he didn't return, we all went to look for him. He was nowhere on the estate—"

"Nonsense, he must be," Maurizio insisted, trying to reassure himself by his own positive voice. In the pause that followed, he could hear Passi gulping, as though trying to pluck up his courage. "Is there more?" he demanded harshly.

"*Signore*—when we first found him gone—we thought—we thought we would find him quickly, and so—"

"*How long has he been gone?*"

Passi gulped again. "Three days," he whispered.

Maurizio gripped the receiver. "It's taken you three days to tell me this?" he demanded.

"No, *signore*," Passi disclaimed frantically. "It was only two days when I called you yesterday morning, but you were away and—and it's three days now," he finished miserably.

"You should have told me at once."

Passi began to gabble. "When we couldn't find him, we searched the roads. Signor Leo was seen boarding a bus on the day he left. I checked his room. His money and some of his clothes were gone."

"Has his memory returned?" Maurizio demanded sharply.

"No. Just a few flashes now and then, but they don't last."

"Which bus did he take?"

"To Rome."

Maurizio felt himself engulfed in a nightmare. In Rome, Leo could vanish without trace. He might remember nothing and never be heard of again. *Or he might remember enough to make him catch a train to Venice.* Maurizio remembered Terri's conviction that she'd seen Leo two days ago. He'd dismissed it, but now he saw she could have been right.

"Send some people to Rome," he commanded. "They must question everyone in the bus station, and then—"

He continued to give orders for several minutes, but he knew it was a forlorn hope, and he was only putting off the moment when he must hang up and find himself alone with the truth: Terri's beloved brother had vanished into the mist, without even a clear idea of his own identity. And he, Maurizio, was to blame. Worse. His servants had delayed telling him for fear of his wrath, thereby losing precious time. For that, too, he was to blame. Was he a monster that people were so terrified of him?

As he replaced the receiver, the silent room seemed to mock his calculations of a few minutes ago. Now his careful plans lay in ruins about him, and he was full of apprehension.

Leo had gone. He was probably already in Venice. Perhaps he would find Terri and tell her everything and he, Maurizio, would be banished from the magic circle that surrounded her. Never again to see the sweet, trusting candor in her eyes or the glow of passion as she reached for him. The thought caused a bitter pain in his heart.

The next moment, he made a sound of impatience with himself. Only action would serve him now.

Ten minutes later, he was on his way to the airport.

Chapter Eight

As soon as she stepped inside the Palazzo Calvani, Terri heard the sound of laughing voices coming from the terrace room. One was Elena's, but the other she didn't recognize.

"Denise has returned," Francisco said. He was just coming out of the library at the rear of the building.

"Denise? You mean Elena's secretary?" Terri asked in dismay. If Denise had returned, then Terri's job here was over, and she'd accomplished nothing. Preoccupied by her love for Maurizio, she'd let the time slip by.

"Yes, but don't worry." Francisco smiled at her. "You can stay here and work for me. Come into the library now and I'll explain what I need." He slipped an arm about her shoulders to guide her to the library. It took all Terri's self-control not to shudder. There was something about Francisco that reminded her of a snake. She managed to slip away from him, smiling to cover the snub, and moved so that he couldn't touch her again. To her relief, Francisco didn't seem offended. If anything, he appeared to be mysteriously pleased by her reserve.

At that moment, Elena appeared. "Terri," she called gaily, "come and have coffee."

Terri looked for Denise as she followed Elena into the terrace room. There was no sign of her, but a door at the far end was just closing. "That's Denise," Elena told her. "She'll be back in a moment."

"If she's returned, you won't need me anymore," Terri said worriedly.

"Oh, but she hasn't returned, not to stay. Her poor mother is more sick than she'd thought at first, so she has to leave me for good. She just came to collect the rest of her clothes."

Terri was swept by relief. "So you still need me?"

Elena gave her warm, sweet smile. "Yes, *cara*, I still need you. Even if Denise had returned, I wouldn't have sent you away because—well, because I wouldn't. See here, I have a surprise for you." She indicated a large box with the name Vilani printed on the side. "Open it," Elena said eagerly, almost as though she were the recipient instead of the giver.

Inside the box, Terri found a blue dress of such elegance and simplicity that she gasped with delight. "But I don't understand," she said. "It's not my birthday—"

"Who cares?" Elena chuckled like a merry child. "Venice is a city of gossip, and the gossip I heard is that you fell into the water and ruined your dress. So you need a new one."

"Elena, it's sweet of you but—"

Elena shrugged. "I like to give you things. Why shouldn't I?"

"Because you already spend too much money on me."

"Too much? *Cara,* whatever are you thinking of? Vilani's clothes cost nothing."

Terri fingered the dress lovingly while her mind reeled from this last statement. A Vilani original couldn't be had for less than five hundred pounds. And Elena thought that was nothing. The Calvani fortune must be even bigger than rumor claimed. The *contessa* read her expression accurately and smiled. "It's nice to be able to have lovely things, isn't it? Don't let your enjoyment be spoiled by guilt. There are so few pleasures in life that we should take them as they come."

"Have you lived like that?" Terri ventured to ask.

"But of course. What other way is there to live?" Elena asked with a pretty shrug. "It's not a matter of money, but of getting the most out of everything that happens to you."

"And of paying the price?" Terri asked cautiously. "Isn't there a saying? Take what you want and pay for it."

Elena's beautiful face clouded for a moment. "Ah, yes," she said on a sigh. "There's always the price. But who can calculate the price until it's too late?" Her look became distant. "And when you're young, it's easy to believe that the day of reckoning will never come," she murmured. "Yet it does come...when you least expect it...." But then, like lightning, she recovered her mood. "So you pay the price and go on. There's always something around the next corner."

"You sound exactly like Leo," Terri said impulsively. "He'll risk everything for the sake of a moment and never count the cost."

Elena considered this with her head to one side. "Am I really like him?" she asked. "Or is it just that he's on your mind, so you see him in everyone?"

"It's true that I can't stop thinking about him," Terri agreed. "I remember him at his best, how he'd laugh off the things that hurt him and always try to see the positive side of any situation. And that's just like you." She hesitated before daring to say, "Didn't you ever realize how alike you were, when you were talking to him?"

"Yes," Elena said slowly. "He was like a kindred spirit. I could say things to Leo that nobody else would understand. He told me how you've always looked after him, and I see it in the way you look after me."

"Oh, I'm more like Papa. He was a very protective person."

"Your face softens when you speak of your father," Elena said, her gaze fixed intently on Terri. "You must have loved him very much."

"I did. If only he hadn't died when we were still so young. It was so lovely to be with him. He used to make silly jokes and laugh at them himself, and you just had to laugh with him."

A gentle smile spread over Elena's face. "Yes," she whispered. "Yes..." A tremor went through her. It seemed to Terri that she made a sudden momentous decision. *"Teresa—"*

A click from the far door made them both look up suddenly. Denise, a tall woman in early middle age, had come quietly into the room. "We were talking about Terri's brother, Leo," Elena said with an effort at casualness that sounded strained. "You met him a few times before you went away."

"A charming young man," Denise said politely. "I hope he's well."

"We don't know," Elena said. "Nobody has seen him for a while, or knows where he is."

"You mean he's disappeared?" Denise frowned. "Have you asked Maurizio about him?"

"Oh, yes," Terri said. "Maurizio remembers having a drink with Leo, but no more."

Denise frowned. "But Maurizio knew your brother better than anyone. They spent a lot of time together."

Terri stared. "Surely you must be wrong. Maurizio knows I'm concerned about Leo. He'd have told me anything he knew."

"Maurizio didn't tell you that Leo spent several weekends at his home in the south?"

Terri had a sudden sensation as if the air was singing in her ears. "His—home—?" she echoed. "You mean—"

"I mean Terranotte. It's an estate near Callena, just outside Rome. He goes down there one weekend a month and I know he took Leo with him a couple of times. In fact—"

"In fact what?" Terri asked, watching Denise's face closely. Her heart was hammering as though she sensed the approach of something too monstrous to contemplate. "Tell me, please."

"The last time I saw Leo, he was at the airport on the day I left Venice. He and Maurizio were flying down to the estate in the helicopter Maurizio used to charter."

"No," Terri said violently. "There must be a mistake. It must have been someone else you saw."

"There's no mistake. Leo came over and talked to me. He was waiting for Maurizio, who'd gone away for a moment to settle some detail with the charter company."

"What did Leo say?" Terri asked in agony.

"We just made small talk for a few minutes. He told me how much he enjoyed his trips to Terranotte. Apparently, he'd been twice before. Then my flight was called and I had to go. I looked back to wave to him but he didn't see me. Maurizio had returned and they were talking."

"You actually saw Maurizio?" Terri said slowly, as though she were trying to comprehend the meaning of her own words.

"Certainly. They were walking away together, talking. I thought nothing of it until now. My mind was taken up with my mother."

Elena frowned. "You left in the third week in September," she said. "And I don't think I ever saw Leo after that. I was surprised because we'd been planning the jewelry project at the art gallery. I thought he must have lost interest and left Venice. He could be wayward."

Terri was fighting not to let her alarm overcome her. There *must* be some rational explanation. And yet, Leo had visited Maurizio's estate and never been seen again. And Maurizio had said nothing to her. Abruptly she turned to Elena. "Did you ever ask Maurizio if Leo had turned up at the casino again?" she demanded.

A change came over Elena. She seemed to flinch. "No, I—I didn't like to."

There was real apprehension in her voice, as though even in his absence Maurizio had the power to frighten her. Terri had seen this reaction before and thought Elena was exaggerating, but now she wondered what else she'd never suspected about him. She loved him, yet suddenly he loomed in her mind as a figure of vague menace, not the tender, passionate lover who'd brought her to life, but a man that people feared—and with good reason.

When Elena spoke again, she seemed to have recovered her confidence. "Teresa, I'm surprised you didn't know all this. You and Maurizio seem so close."

"Yes," Terri said heavily. "Seemed."

For the rest of the day, she functioned on automatic while her divided self argued, one half refusing to believe that Maurizio had been deceiving her, the other half full of dread for what she would discover next. Elena sent her home early, and as soon as Terri reached the Midas, she consulted a map of Italy. She found Callena easily. It was about ten miles outside Rome.

A resolution was growing within her. She called Elena and asked for the next few days off. "Have you asked Maurizio about Leo?" Elena said.

"I can't. He's at Terranotte. I have to go there myself and find out what's been happening."

"Terri, be careful. Maurizio is a dangerous man."

"I think I've always known that," Terri said somberly. "But I can't believe—there must be some innocent explanation."

"You'd better go. But please be careful."

By twelve o'clock that evening, Terri was on the night train to Rome. She lay awake all night in her sleeper, listening to the rhythm of the wheels while her thoughts went around and around like a mouse trapped on a treadmill. It wasn't possible—but Maurizio had spoken of needing her forgiveness. What was the truth about this man whom everyone seemed to fear? *What did she need to forgive?*

At dawn, she had her breakfast at a little café on the main concourse of Rome station, and by the time she'd finished, the offices were beginning to open for the day. She bought a map of the area and hired a car to take her to Callena. It turned out to be a small village, and the first man she stopped directed her to Terranotte.

Her heart was beating madly as she drove the last few miles. Surely she would soon awake and find it had all been a nightmare. But as the miles vanished beneath the wheels and still she didn't awaken, her face grew more set and determined.

At last she saw the place she was looking for, a rambling yellow stone villa with a red-tiled roof, surrounded by bougainvillea. She drove through the wide arched gate and brought the car to an abrupt halt. As she jumped out, a man came forward and with horror she saw that he had a large gap between his two front teeth, just like the man who'd gone to the Busoni to pay Leo's bill and collect his things. "Where is he?" Terri screamed at him.

The man frowned and stared. Terri dodged around him and ran into the house, her shoes echoing on the tiled floor. "Leo—" she called. *"Leo—"*

Only silence answered her. She ran upstairs and began to look in room after room, crying his name, but there was no sign of him. Then, in the last room, she stopped and stared while her stomach churned and terror grew in her.

It was an empty bedroom. The bed was stripped and the room was bare, but a wardrobe door had swung open and inside Terri could see a dark blue shirt that she recognized. She'd given it to Leo last Christmas. "Oh, dear God!" she whispered. She pulled the shirt off the hanger and clutched it to her, as if she could somehow make contact with her brother. "Leo, what's happened to you?"

She became aware of a shadow in the doorway and whirled to confront Maurizio. "Where is he?" she screamed. *"What have you done with him?"*

Maurizio was very pale beneath his tan. "I'd give anything for you not to have found out like this."

"Found out what? What have you been keeping from me?"

"Teresa, please listen to me—"

Terri cast aside the shirt and ran to seize Maurizio by the shoulders. "Where is he?" she cried, shaking him. "What have you done with him?"

"Nothing, I swear it."

"Where *is* he?"

Maurizio took a long, ragged breath. "I don't know."

"Don't lie to me. Haven't you told me enough lies?"

"I'm not lying," he said desperately. "I've no idea where Leo is."

"Are you going to pretend that he wasn't here?"

"No. He was here, but he left four days ago."

"Where did he go?"

"I don't know. He didn't tell anyone he was going—just slipped away."

"What was he doing here all this time? Didn't you tell him I was looking for him?"

"Teresa, please don't rush to judge me," Maurizio begged. "Nothing is the way it looks. Leo has been ill. He was here on a visit when he came down with a fever. I got him the best medical attention to be had—a doctor and two nurses doing shifts around the clock. They pulled him through but—"

"But what?" Terri asked wildly.

"But when his fever abated, he—he wasn't quite himself. Physically he's strong again but his mind wanders."

"What do you mean—wanders?" she demanded, aghast.

"He doesn't know who he is. Sometimes he seems on the verge of remembering, but then the moment passes. Mostly his mind is filled with confusion."

"Oh, my God!" Terri wept. "Poor Leo. I could have helped him. If he'd seen me, everything could have come back to him. Why didn't you tell me he was here?"

Maurizio took a deep breath. "That's a long story, and I want you to listen to me carefully."

"Oh, I'll listen all right. Because I'm fascinated to know what kind of explanation you can offer for concealing Leo from me. And all the time you—we—" She choked with bitter memory.

"That had nothing to do with it," he said harshly. "What happened between us was—was something separate."

"Separate? How could it be? I'm not like you. I can't keep my life in neatly packaged compartments. I could never deceive you as you've deceived me because I—" She shuddered.

"Because you what?"

"Never mind. Whatever there was, is all over now. Did you enjoy tricking me, all the time knowing you had Leo here in secret?"

"You don't understand."

"No, and I never will. What kind of man could behave as you've done? What kind of man *are* you, Maurizio."

"I don't know," he said hoarsely. "A madman, perhaps. If my behavior seems strange to you—it seems stranger to me. But I was driven by things you know nothing of."

"Yes, I'm starting to realize that I've never known anything where you were concerned," she said. "It was all planned, wasn't it? The room that was 'overbooked' so that I'd be put into a better one—you wanted me to stay, and making me comfortable was one way of ensuring it. And the day I went to the Busoni and you appeared out of nowhere. That wasn't a coincidence. You followed me there to keep tabs on me and find out how much I'd learned. It's all been a careful front to deceive me."

He was shocked to hear her put it like that, but mostly shocked by the realization that she was right. It had started out that way. Yet that seemed so long ago, in another life, before he'd discovered her beauty of body and spirit and felt his heart thawing to new life. He felt as though he were standing on the edge of a precipice, trying not to glance down at what awaited him if he made a clumsy move, knowing he had no choice but to begin the perilous crossing. "Teresa, please be calm and hear me out."

"Calm?" she echoed bitterly. "I don't feel as if I could ever be calm again."

"But it's only in calmness that you could hope to understand," he said desperately. "Try to set aside your anger while I explain."

But she clung to her anger, knowing that she needed it. If anger evaporated, it would leave a vacuum that would be filled by grief, agonizing grief that the man who'd brought her heart and body to life had been wearing a mask. And behind that mask was a cold-hearted schemer. She looked at Maurizio from hard eyes. "All right" she said. "I'm as calm as I'll ever be. Explain."

"Not here—not like this."

"Now," she said in a voice of iron.

To his horror, Maurizio found himself struggling for words. He'd always been the man in command while others were at a disadvantage, but now it was hard to speak under the gaze of her accusing eyes. He drew a deep breath. "In the beginning," he said, "it all seemed so straightforward—a simple matter of revenge."

"Revenge? Against Leo? Against me? What have we ever done to you?"

"Nothing. But your mother has done me great harm."

"My mother?"

"Elena Calvani."

She stared at him in horror. "You knew she was my mother? You've known all this time?"

"Leo told me everything one evening when he'd had too much to drink. I've hated Elena ever since she drove my brother to his death. I'd lived for revenge, and suddenly I saw how to achieve it."

"By spiriting Leo away?"

"I told you that was an accident. Leo became ill while he was here."

"And you made use of his illness?" she asked scornfully.

"That's not true. I thought only of getting him well."

"So he was more use to you alive than dead?"

Maurizio clenched his hands. He didn't know how to deal with her jeering accusations. "I thought only of getting him well," he repeated. "It wasn't until he was out of danger and I returned to Venice that I saw—" He stopped, realizing that whatever he said next, she would despise him.

"Well? What did you see?"

"That Elena was worried. He'd never told her who he was but I believe she guessed. And when he disappeared from Venice—"

"You used it to torment her."

"Yes," he shouted. "Just as she tormented my poor brother, through his love for her, tormented him until he couldn't endure life any longer and went to his death—a death she could have prevented. Don't judge me. There's too much you can't comprehend."

"How convenient," she snapped. "What a perfect excuse for despicable behavior."

He was deadly pale. "Teresa, I warn you—"

"You warn me?" she echoed incredulously. "Who do you think you are to warn me? Because of you, Leo is sick, lost, maybe in danger. You might at least have kept him safe."

"I thought he was safe. I gave orders that he was to be watched at all times for his own protection, but somehow he managed to slip away."

She turned away from him and sat down on the bed, clutching Leo's shirt to her as if it were a talisman. "It was him I saw, wasn't it?" she asked, dazed. "On the bridge in Venice—it was him."

"I don't know. It might have been."

"It was him—as you knew it was. You kept saying it couldn't be him—but you knew."

"No," he said quickly. "I didn't know he'd left here. I didn't find out until afterward."

She looked at him from stony eyes. "I don't believe you. He must have been missing for at least a day by then. You knew it could be him."

"No, because—"

"Because what?" An ironic note came into Terri's voice. "Surely you can tell me anything now? What can be worse than what I've already discovered?"

"All right. My people here didn't try to contact me until three days after he'd gone."

Terri considered this in silence before nodding. "They were afraid to tell you, weren't they?" she demanded bitterly.

"Yes, I think they were," he admitted.

"I asked you what kind of man you were. I should have said what kind of devil?"

He was silent. He couldn't plead for her understanding again. He could see himself through her honest, steadfast eyes and the sight filled him with shame.

Terri rose. "I'm going back to Venice," she said. "Leo's there somewhere and I'm going to find him."

"My helicopter can be ready to leave in half an hour," Maurizio said. "I'll take you back and we'll search for Leo together."

Terri looked at him. Her eyes were no longer stones. Rather, they had a hazy look of distance as though she could see right through him. The sight gave Maurizio an unnerving sensation, as if he actually wasn't there, or as if he was a man with nothing but emptiness inside. "Don't come near me," she said in a voice that chilled him. "Don't touch me, don't even talk to me until I say you can."

Terri herself couldn't have said where that sudden assumption of authority had come from. She only knew that a change had come over her, turning her into another person. She wasn't sure she liked the new woman who was filled with hate and scorn. But she was also filled with strength, and Terri knew she was going to need that strength. "If any harm comes to Leo, it will be your fault," she said. "I'm going now. Don't try to stop me. You wouldn't like it if I spoke my mind in front of your servants."

He made no attempt to detain her. He seemed too stunned to move. Terri descended the stairs at a steady pace. She didn't look around her but she was intensely aware of curious eyes following her every movement. Ignoring them, she went out to the car and drove quickly away.

She didn't head straight back to Rome, but went out into the countryside and stopped where there was no one around. She needed to be alone with the turmoil in her brain. She got out of the car and walked around for a while, but her thoughts refused to compose themselves. Now the thing she'd feared was happening, and grief was taking over: grief for Leo and grief for the shattering of her newborn love. She buried her face against a tree and gave herself up to the sobs that racked her. Every inch of her seemed to have come alive with the memory of the passion that she'd learned in Maurizio's arms. He'd touched her body and her heart and made them both sing, but now she must order them to be silent, and the command was agony. He'd deceived her. She'd been nothing but a part of his plan for revenge, and the love she'd thought had flowered between them was hollow and false. She wept until she was weary. But then she dried her tears and swore that she wouldn't weep again. From now on, only strength was any use to her. She got in the car and drove to Rome.

She arrived too late for the afternoon train, so she booked herself a berth on the night sleeper and went to have a meal. She wasn't hungry but she forced the food down grimly.

She expected to sleep badly, if at all, but the feeling of having made a decision seemed to have relaxed her. She dozed off quickly, sleeping until the train was about to pull into Venice. She was a different person from the shy, uncertain young woman who'd first arrived in Venice. Now she went to the vaporetto stop and stepped confidently onto the first boat that arrived. She didn't sit down but stood in the prow until they neared the Midas, and then she was the first off. At the hotel she instructed the receptionist to prepare her bill, and hurried up to her room. She wanted to be packed and out of here before Maurizio tried to intercept her.

But as soon as she threw open her door, she froze at the sight of Maurizio standing by the window, his face haggard as if he were being tormented by the Furies themselves.

Chapter Nine

"I might have known," she said contemptuously.

"I flew back yesterday afternoon. I went to the station to meet the evening train. When you weren't on it, I didn't know what to think."

The words didn't begin to describe the abyss of fear that had opened up in him at the thought that she, too, might have vanished. It had taken several minutes before he'd calmed down enough to remember a friend in the travel industry who owed him a favor. The friend had checked with Rome, discovering that Terri was on the sleeper, and the relief that filled Maurizio had been like a warning of the uncharted seas that surrounded him. He'd tried to resist the knowledge, telling himself that no woman had ever mattered that much and no woman ever would. In this mood he'd returned to the Midas. But then the fear had flooded back, driving him to go to her room so that he didn't miss her. "But now you're here, there are many things we must discuss," he said.

"I've got nothing more to say to you," Terri said briskly. "I'm moving out of the Midas."

"The hell you are!" he said violently. "Where do you think you're going?"

"I don't *think* anything, Maurizio. I'm simply leaving, whether you like it or not. Unlike everyone else, I'm not afraid of you."

Maurizio swore softly, more at himself than anyone else. "I didn't mean to sound like that. Please, Teresa, don't do anything in a hurry. We have to talk."

"I'll talk when I'm ready. In the meantime, I have packing to do."

"But where will you go?"

"I'll find somewhere. There are plenty of rooms. Please step aside so that I can get to my things."

He did so and stood watching her as she moved about. His expression was baffled. "I've never seen you so hard and cold before."

"I've never had such cause before, but you'd better get used to me as I am, because this is it for the future."

"I don't believe you. The gentle, beautiful woman who lay in my arms could never have turned into this."

"Don't you ever speak of that again," she cried passionately. "That woman didn't exist, any more than you—" She stopped and took a shuddering breath. Suddenly, her eyes were blurred but she brushed a hand over them and went on with her packing, her jaw set.

"I swear to you that when we lay together, there was only truth between us," Maurizio said earnestly.

She confronted him. "If you want me to believe a word you say, there's a simple way to do it. Find my brother. Let me hear from his own lips that you didn't harm him, and then maybe I can forgive you."

"I'm doing all I can to find Leo. I've got people tearing Venice apart but—"

"But it's a good place for a man to vanish," she finished for him. "Especially one who doesn't know who he is. Anything could have happened to him. He might have fallen into a canal the way I did, and perhaps there was no one to help him out." She saw by his ravaged face that this was his greatest dread, and felt a bitter satisfaction at his suffering. An imp of cruelty possessed her. If he could be a devil, so could she. "We'd never know, would we, Maurizio? A stranger to Venice, slipping beneath the water, leaving no gap because no one knew his name. Just something for you to wonder about for the rest of your life." Her voice broke. "And for me to wonder about, too. What did Leo or I ever do to you that you should be so cruel?"

"I told you it wasn't you," he said violently. "It was Elena Calvani."

"You don't evade your responsibilities that easily."

Maurizio's face set grimly. "I'm not trying to evade my responsibilities. What I did was wrong and I'm trying to put it right, but there's more than one side to this."

"I don't believe you."

"Then I'll have to show you," he said, seizing her hand and heading for the door.

"Let go of me," Terri said, trying to pull away.

"Not until you've seen what I want you to. Then maybe things won't look so simple to you."

She gave up the struggle and let Maurizio take her downstairs to the landing stage. He dismissed his boatman with a brief gesture and handed her in, starting the engine at once and heading out into the Grand Canal. She was assailed by the memory of the last time they'd been in this boat together. That had been only a few days ago, yet in that short time the world had turned upside down, pitchforking her from heaven into hell. For a moment, her grief welled up again and threatened to overwhelm her, but she crushed it with a terrible effort. "It won't make any difference, Maurizio," she said.

"Wait before you say that."

He took the boat out into the lagoon and swung left. "I don't want to go back to Murano," she insisted.

"We're not going to Murano," he told her. Then she realized that he was heading for San Michele, the walled island she'd noticed on the first journey, the place he'd called the cemetery of Venice. In a few minutes, he'd tied up at the landing stage and they were walking through the dark portals. It was like no cemetery she'd ever seen. "Venetians are buried above ground because of the water," Maurizio informed her. "Coffins are placed in marble vaults, in slots side by side and tier on tier."

The tiers rose above her head and stretched away in long blocks. Coffins were pushed in headfirst, and at the foot of each one, a plate of marble had been fitted in, sealing it off. Each plate contained an urn for flowers so that the effect was of a wall of flowers. Where two such walls faced each other, there was a corridor of blooms.

Maurizio led her down two corridors, striding ahead in a manner that showed he was heading for a familiar spot. Terri guessed what was coming and tried to harden her mind to resist what she saw as manipulation, but she couldn't help being curious. At last they stopped at the end of a corridor and Maurizio indicated three plaques. Terri studied them, noting the names: Annunciata and Pietro Vanzani, Maurizio's parents. Below them was the memorial of Rufio Vanzani, who'd died earlier that year, aged twenty-three.

Beside the urn a photograph had been imprinted in the marble. Terri looked closely and saw a charming young man with a bright, eager expression. The handsome face seemed so full of life that she almost expected him to speak to her. She glanced at Maurizio, seeing the brotherly likeness in their features. Yet there were vital differences. Rufio had a ready smile and he looked as if he'd found life kind and generous. On Maurizio's face, the harsh lines had settled long ago, and as he gazed at the picture, his eyes held a dark, brooding melancholy.

"He looks delightful," Terri said.

"He *was* delightful. He was in love with life and, God help him, he was in love with *her*."

"By 'her,' I suppose you mean Elena," Terri said tartly. "There's no need to speak of her as if she were Messalina."

"Messalina," Maurizio echoed. "Now there's an excellent description that I hadn't thought of. Messalina, a cruel and corrupt woman who played with men's hearts for pleasure and tossed them aside when they grew inconvenient."

"I don't believe my mother is like that."

"How do you know what she's like? She played love games with Rufio, but they weren't games to him. He was madly in love with her. He dreamed of their making a life together. What delusions! As though the woman who'd sold herself to the most corrupt man in Venice for the sake of his wealth and title could ever have lived on love in a cottage.

"When he begged her to come away with him, she ended their affair at once. His love made him a threat to her position. Her rejection plunged him into black despair and he killed himself."

"And you blame Elena for that?"

"Not just for that. She knew what he was going to do—"

"You can't be sure—"

"But I can. He left me a letter, saying that he'd told her he was going to end his life, but she'd simply ignored him. She could have stopped him but she didn't bother. Why should she? His death removed an inconvenience. For this, I will never forgive or forget."

"So all this is for vengeance," Terri said bitterly.

"For vengeance," he confirmed. *"Per vendetta."*

"It's horrible."

"It's inevitable. Do you think I'd let her get away with it? Rufio was worth more than that."

"So that's how you justify the unjustifiable," she snapped. "What gives you the right to punish her?"

"The fact that nobody else ever will," he growled. "And when Leo came here and I discovered the truth, at last I saw my way. You can be sure Elena never told her husband she had twins by another man. He wants a son. He'd love an excuse to be rid of her and she knows it."

"So why didn't you just just tell Francisco? Or was that too simple? Yes, that's it. You've enjoyed watching Elena on hot coals. You've relished working in the shadows, creating an atmosphere of fear. You're a monster."

"Don't expect me to feel guilty about how I treat a murderess. Vendetta is an old and honorable Italian custom. Your blood is Italian, Teresa. It speaks to you of things others could never understand. Listen to it."

"Yes, my blood is Italian," Terri retorted. "But my rearing was English and vendetta means nothing to me."

He took hold of her shoulders. "Listen to me—" He checked himself, staring over her shoulder. Terri turned to see what had caught his attention, and down the long avenue of flowers she saw a delicate woman, dressed in black, with blond hair, coming toward them. "Elena!" Maurizio breathed. Swiftly he drew Terri aside.

Elena walked with her eyes cast down and a grave, sad expression on her face. Her clothes were black, which made Maurizio's lips curl in derision. "Such hypocrisy!" he muttered.

"You make easy judgments," Terri snapped.

Elena approached the plaque and stopped to gaze at it. In her hands she had a small posy of flowers and she proceeded to add them to the flowers already in the urn. Then she laid her fingertips gently against Rufio's picture and murmured softly, "I'm sorry. I'm so sorry." There were tears in her eyes.

Terri stepped forward, shaking off Maurizio's hand. "No," she said furiously. "Too much has happened in the shadows. It's time your hatred was dragged into the light."

The sound of her voice made Elena look up. She smiled at the sight of Terri but her expression changed to one of horror when she saw Maurizio watching her. "M-Maurizio," she stammered. "I—I came to—"

"To ask forgiveness of the boy you killed?" Maurizio finished coldly. "How convenient that he can't answer you, so you can imagine a reply that suits you. But *I* speak for Rufio and I tell you that *I* do not forgive. Nor do I forget, *contessa*. Remember that."

Elena had flinched but then she seemed to gather her courage to answer him with spirit. "I know you'll never forgive me," she said. "You were always pitiless. But Rufio wasn't like you. He was generous and kind, and he would have forgiven me."

"What man forgives the woman who kills him?" Maurizio demanded.

"I didn't kill Rufio," Elena said emotionally.

"You knew he was suicidal and you let him die."

"But I *didn't* know."

"In his last letter to me, he said he'd told you—"

"It's not true," Elena cried.

"Rufio was never a liar. He said he told you and I believe him. No doubt you had your own reasons for keeping silent."

"If I'd known, I would have tried to stop him, I swear it," Elena cried. "I'd never have hurt Rufio. I—I..." she checked herself.

"Surely you won't dare to say you loved him?" Maurizio jeered.

"I—I was very fond of him," Elena faltered. "He was a dear boy. When he started flirting with me, I thought it was just a game."

"As it was to you."

"I never knew he took it so seriously until—until it was too late. Oh, God!" Elena buried her face in her hands and wept. Terri put her arms around her, and Elena instinctively turned toward her.

But Maurizio didn't soften. "What a pretty performance!" he said harshly. "But my brother still lies buried in that marble because you were heartless."

"If there was anything I could do to bring him back..." Elena sobbed. "But I can't—*I can't.*"

"No, you can't," Maurizio agreed. "And so events must take their course, *contessa.*"

Elena looked up imploringly but Maurizio's expression was stony. With a little cry, she turned and fled. Terri didn't try to follow her. She would comfort Elena later. First, she had unfinished business to take care of.

Maurizio glowered at Terri. "You shouldn't have done that," he said. "Do you think you've made things any better?"

"I've forced you out into the open where at least she can see you working against her."

"Just how open do you mean to be? Are you going to tell her who you are?"

She took a long breath. "I don't know. I sometimes wonder if she guesses."

He nodded. "Perhaps she doesn't want to know. You're as much of a threat to her as I am—as Rufio was."

"At any rate, you must see now that she's not as heartless as you thought. She's truly sorry about Rufio's death."

"Then she should have prevented it when she had the chance."

"But you heard her say—"

"Yes, I heard her and I didn't believe a word of it. Such a pretty performance, including flowers for effect." Maurizio began to strip away the flowers Elena had placed in the urn, but Terri seized his hands.

"Stop it!" she said fiercely. "She meant well, but you're so eaten up with hate and mistrust that you can't see anyone straight."

"I thought I saw *you* straight," he retorted. "But now I see you siding with my enemy."

"I'm not siding with your enemy, Maurizio. I *am* your enemy. I thought I loved you, but now I see there's no one there to love, just a shell with nothing inside but revenge. I thought you loved me, but you can't love anyone."

He flinched as if she'd struck him. "Have you finished?" he demanded coldly.

"Yes, except for this. Find my brother and restore him to me safely. Otherwise, I'll remember the lesson you've taught me about vendetta."

She turned and ran away from him. A public motor boat had arrived at the landing stage and she hurried onto it. As it drew away into the lagoon, she saw Maurizio emerge, looking for her. She watched as the distance between them grew. In her morbid state, that growing width of water seemed symbolic. Her heart felt like lead within her but her jaw was set. She would not let herself weaken now.

At the hotel she hurried upstairs and packed as quickly as she could, throwing her clothes in with no concern to orderliness. As she was closing the last lock, there was a knock at the door. "Who is it?" she called cautiously.

"Francisco."

Surprised, she opened the door to the count. "Elena told me everything that happened at the cemetery," he said. "I hurried here at once."

"I'm leaving the Midas. I can't stay here with Maurizio, not after he—" Abruptly, she stopped speaking, realizing that she couldn't tell the whole story without betraying Elena's secret.

"Yes?" Francisco urged, watching her face.

"After he behaved so cruelly to Elena," Terri finished lamely.

Francisco studied her for a moment longer, then he said, "I know about Rufio. Venice is a city of love and these little flirtations are innocent enough. It's a tragedy that Rufio took it so seriously, but I've told Elena she mustn't blame herself. She came home very upset, so I've come to fetch you. You must stay with us now."

"You mean live in the palazzo?

"Elena needs you. I know you won't refuse her this little service. If you've finished your packing, we could go now." He took her bags and they went out together.

At the reception desk, she received a shock. Francisco had already paid her bill. "I was simply acting on my wife's instructions," he said. "Now, let's go."

In a few moments, her bags were loaded into his motorboat and they were moving. As they swung out into the Grand Canal, Maurizio's boat appeared, but he didn't see them.

At the palazzo, Elena greeted her by running down the full length of the grand stairway and throwing her arms about Terri's neck. "Thank you for coming," she whispered. "Promise not to leave me."

"I promise," Terri said. "Let's go upstairs."

Once in her own room, Elena almost collapsed, clinging to Terri and shaking like a leaf. "I knew he hated me," she said through streaming tears. "But not that much." She buried her face against Terri, sobbing hysterically, and for the moment there was nothing Terri could do but hold her and try to comfort her. She put her arms about Elena and sat beside her on the bed, rocking her as though she were the mother and Elena her child.

At last Elena raised her head. Her hair was in disarray and her makeup smudged. The perfectly groomed beauty had vanished, to be replaced by a tortured, despairing woman. "I didn't know what Rufio was going to do," she moaned. "He never told me he was thinking of suicide, I swear he didn't. Oh, Teresa, you must believe me."

"Of course I believe you."

"I don't understand why Rufio should tell his brother such a lie. He'd never have hurt me."

"Did you love him?" Terri asked gently.

"How could I help but love him? He loved me and I was so lonely for love. But I was so much older. If we'd lived together, he'd soon have realized it was a mistake, but his honor would have made him stay with me. His life would have been ruined. I loved him too dearly to do that to him. I tried to explain why we had no future but he wouldn't listen. He just kept saying that I couldn't love him. I thought he'd understand one day. I never dreamed—" She burst into more sobs and Terri enfolded her again in her arms, hating Maurizio. How could a man cause such devastation and still try to justify himself?

At last Elena pulled herself together and took Terri to the room she'd had prepared for her. Terri looked around her in amazement. It was almost as luxurious as Elena's own, not at all the room of a paid employee. "I don't need anything as grand as this—"

"But this is close to my room," Elena said eagerly. "I need you near me. I feel stronger if you're there."

"Of course, if that's what you want."

Suddenly, they both tensed. From somewhere deep in the house they could hear the sound of doors banging, men's voices raised in anger. Terri slipped out onto the landing and looked down the long stairs to where she could see Francisco and another man. The painful thump of her heart told her the other man's identity before she could see his face. For an instant, she was on the verge of returning to her room, locking the door and staying there, where Maurizio couldn't get her. But the next moment, her head went up and she was walking purposefully down the stairs to confront him.

"I'm glad to see you, *signorina*," Francisco said. "Our friend here seems to think I kidnapped you. Perhaps you can enlighten him."

Maurizio ignored him and strode up to Terri. "Come away from here," he said urgently. "It's no place for you."

"On the contrary," she said, "it's the ideal place. I'm close to my work and Elena needs me."

"I'm sure you'd prefer to talk in private," Francisco said with a cool smile. "Oblige me by making use of my study." He indicated the double doors immediately behind her, and walked away.

Maurizio followed her into Francisco's study and closed the heavy doors. "You have to leave here," he insisted. "I know Francisco better than you. The most corrupt, debauched sinner in all Venice, a man with no morals and no scruples, whose pastime is destroying innocence—''

"You had no scruples about introducing me to him for your own purposes," she reminded him pointedly.

He winced. "I never liked your working here, but as long as you weren't living under his roof—''

Terri swung around to face him, eyes blazing. "Do you think I do only what *you* allow? Oh, yes—you had a plan. Leo and I were to be your pawns, but we both spoiled it by doing things you hadn't thought of, didn't we? Now we've stepped out of your plan. Leo is wandering around somewhere, not knowing who he is, and I've come to where I belong.''

"You don't know what you're saying,'' he said desperately. "You don't belong in this sink of corruption.''

"Who isn't corrupt? You with your heartless scheming? Not me, surely? I've been taught some fascinating lessons by a man who took my heart and twisted it to his own purpose, a man who degraded love by using it as a weapon in the vendetta. Can anyone be more corrupt than that? Why are you here, Maurizio? Why aren't you out looking for my brother?''

"I'm going to find him if I have to tear this city apart.''

"Then do it. And when you've done it, come back and I may have something to say to you.''

"I don't know you,'' he said, staring at her, dazed. "It can't be you, speaking like this.''

"It's me as I am now. You said I'd discover myself in Venice and I have. And I like the new me. She's strong enough to cope with what you've done and tell you to go to hell."

"It can't end between us like this—"

"It's already ended."

"And what we were to each other—can you forget it just like that?"

"We were nothing to each other," she cried in anguish. "I thought—you made me think—" She choked and brought herself under control by sheer force of will. Devastated, paralyzed with horror, Maurizio couldn't tear his eyes from the havoc he'd wreaked. His lips formed her name but he could make no sound. "None of that matters," she said when she could trust her voice. "I thought you were an honest man. You thought I was a fool. We were both wrong."

"We thought many things about each other, Teresa," he said somberly. "And some of them were true."

"Nothing was true," she said vehemently. "Not one word from the beginning. You planned everything so that I could be useful to you in your plan. Even when—" She broke off, shuddering.

"Teresa." He came toward her.

"No, don't come near me. I never want to see you again unless it's to tell me that Leo's safe."

"I'll find him," he swore. "But, Teresa I beg you to believe that my feelings for you have been honest."

"Oh, I do. Vengeance is a very honest feeling," she raged.

"For God's sake, don't make this worse by denying the truth of what's between us."

"I decide my own truth," she retorted. "I'll never again take 'the truth' from you."

"Not from me but from your own heart. It speaks for me, Teresa. Listen to it."

"My heart speaks only of hatred," she said bitterly. "There's nothing else there."

"I don't believe you," he said, coming very close to her.

She saw what he meant to do and put up a hand to ward him off, but he ignored it and pulled her close. She refused to struggle, but looked up at him with fierce eyes. Her breast rose and fell quickly with her anger and she could hear his heart hammering against her, but she felt none of the old tenderness. Hatred as strong as passion welled up within her, making her breath come quickly and her eyes glitter. That sight was Maurizio's undoing. With a growl, he tightened his arms and dropped his head to lay his lips on hers.

She tensed, holding herself motionless, fighting him with silence and stillness. Let him see that he had no power over her now.

If only it were true. Within seconds, she knew that her hatred and her new strength were useless against the passion that his lightest touch could bring alive. And he wasn't touching her lightly now, but with purpose and a determination to make her relive everything she wanted to forget. His lips were torturers invoking the memory of suffocating kisses that had led to deeper delight. His hands were possessed by black magic, recalling caresses that had driven her wild when they lay together—as they never would again.

"No," she whispered, unable to endure the memory. *"No."*

"There are some truths that are beyond words, Teresa," he growled against her lips. "Love me or hate me—as long as I live in your heart somehow."

He smothered her answer beneath a kiss that burned her with its wildness. His mouth was desperate as it strove to reawaken the tenderness and delight that had once been his for the taking. All tenderness was gone from the woman in his arms now. Her eyes, blazing up into his, were hostile, but even in the midst of hostility there was a gleam of something no hatred could kill, something that had existed between man and woman since the dawn of time. Part of her was still his and would always be his. But he knew this wasn't enough. He could rekindle her passion but not her love, and now that he'd thrown it away forever, he understood that it was her love he wanted. This one woman, so different from any other, had been sent by an ironic fate to torment him. He'd meant to use her but she'd turned the tables on him, showing him how little he knew of the human heart, reducing him to despair.

"Love me or hate me," he repeated.

"Let it be hate then," she said fiercely.

"You don't know what you're saying! Do you think there can ever be any feeling between us that isn't infused with passion?"

"I can be as passionate when I hate as when I love. Hate can be beautiful, Maurizio. It sings in my blood and shows me how to enjoy your pain and fear. And you *are* afraid, aren't you? You're afraid that Leo may never be found. But why should you worry? If he's dead, you'll have the final revenge on Elena. You'll enjoy that, won't you?"

"No," he cried hoarsely.

"But you should. It'll be the perfect murder, because nobody will ever be able to prove his death was your fault. They'll suspect. I'll make sure of that. They'll wonder every time they look at you, but there'll never be any proof. You'll stay free, but for the rest of your life, Leo's ghost will walk one step behind you."

"Did a devil put those words in your mouth?" he demanded. "Do you enjoy tormenting me?"

"Yes, I enjoy it."

He stood back and regarded her in horror. "I've committed many crimes," he said, "but I think the greatest one is the change I've wrought in you. Dear God, what have I done to you—to us?"

"What have you done to me? You've taken my brother away from me, perhaps destroyed him. In here—" she laid her hands over her heart "—you've so changed me that I don't know myself. I only know I'll never be the same person again."

"I regret that most of all," he said somberly. "The woman you were was gentle and kind—and lovable. She made me think that perhaps we—"

"Don't!" she cried in agony. "That's all over. It was never more than an illusion."

"Perhaps love itself is an illusion. Perhaps it's an illusion that one person is different from any other. I only know that for me you *were* different. No other woman has ever been like you. No other woman has touched my heart."

She backed away from him, hands covering her ears. Her eyes were wild for his words seemed to her a monstrous cruelty. "Stop it!" she cried. "*Stop it.* Don't ever speak to me this way again."

He took a step toward her. She warded him off. The next moment, she was running out of the room, out of the palazzo, running into the streets of Venice where there was anonymity and escape from words of love that were the most terrible she'd ever heard.

Chapter Ten

Terri ran without looking where she was going, but soon realized that she was taking the old route to the Midas, and turned aside sharply. After a while, she knew she was lost. The back streets of Venice were all so similar that it was like wandering in a maze. Wherever she turned, she found the same flagstones, the same narrow, dimly lit alleys and shuttered windows. She tried to retrace her steps but the route she'd just traveled had vanished as if by magic, replaced by streets she could have sworn she'd never seen before, although they were all so alike.

She quickened her pace, desperately seeking some place that she recognized. Little canals appeared, crossed by toy bridges that vanished under her feet, each one like the last. The streets grew narrower, the buildings rearing over her head until they seemed to touch one another. This was the Venice she'd been warned of, the place of shadows and sinister magic. The whole city conspired against her, leading her in dark circles. She looked up wildly at the blind windows. Perhaps Leo was behind one of them, hidden away in fear and confusion.

"Leo," she cried. *"Leo—where are you?"*

Shutters creaked, heads appeared, faces full of kindly concern, but she was running again, gone before anyone could help her. Those who looked out saw only an empty street, heard far off the mournful echo, "Leo—Leo—" and shut themselves into the warm again, thinking they'd heard one of the ghosts whose shades had lingered in the corners of Venice throughout long centuries.

But one man knew it was no ghost. He followed the sound determinedly through twisting ways until at last he caught up with Terri, leaning against a wall, shivering. "Now, what possessed you to run out without a coat in the middle of winter?" he demanded.

Startled, Terri looked up, and saw Bruno. "I forgot I wasn't wearing a coat," she said tiredly. He pulled off his own jacket and tried to put it around her shoulders, but she drew away and regarded him with suspicion. "Did you know?" she demanded.

He didn't waste time asking what she meant. "I knew Maurizio hated Elena and saw you as part of his revenge," he admitted. "I tried to hint to you that things weren't all they seemed, although I lacked the courage to say it outright. But then I saw him falling in love with you, and thought it would be all right."

"All right? When he was concealing Leo?"

"I didn't know about that, I swear it. Not until the day before yesterday. If I'd known, I'd have told you everything, despite Maurizio."

After a moment, Terri nodded. "I believe you." She let him drape his jacket about her sagging shoulders.

"Let's get you back to the Midas," he said.

"I'm not staying at the Midas anymore," she said quickly. "I've moved into the Palazzo Calvani."

"I see," he said. "Was that wise?"

"It was inevitable."

"Well, let's get you into the warm, wherever it is."

He guided her through a couple of small streets and suddenly there was the Grand Canal. Terri was amazed to find she'd been so close to it all the time. A vaporetto was just pulling in to a landing stage and he hurried her onto it and stayed with her throughout the journey.

Elena saw them coming from an upstairs window and hurried down to the door. "Get her to bed quickly, she's taken cold," Bruno said, and slipped away.

Elena immediately took charge of her, drawing her up to her room and helping her to undress, clucking like a protective hen. The cold seemed to have penetrated Terri's bones and she couldn't stop shivering, even when she was in the warm bed. "I'm sorry to give you so much trouble," she muttered.

To her surprise, Elena smiled. "You're no trouble. I'm going to enjoy myself."

"*You* can't take care of me," Terri said, scandalized.

"Why not? Leave me to do the worrying."

Terri gave up. Her head was aching and all she wanted to do was sleep. She sank into a fevered dream in which Madge seemed to be there with her, saying with a sneer, "I told you so. Slut!" Madge had been right all the time. Terri had given her love to a man who was only using her. She was a *slut* and love was vile, after all. The discovery made her cry out with anguish, and suddenly someone was there, comforting her, cooling her forehead and speaking soft words. She opened her eyes and found Elena leaning over her. The countess was dressed in nightclothes and her hair hung about her face, as though she'd had no time to worry about her appearance. She looked softer without her mask of glamour.

Over the next few days, she tended Terri at all hours, bringing her meals, some of which she'd cooked herself. It was blissful to be cared for so tenderly. During Terri's childhood illnesses, Madge had nursed her conscientiously but had never made her feel cherished and cocooned in affection as Elena did.

One day when Terri had merely toyed with a tempting meal, Elena gathered some on a spoon and said firmly, "Just one more mouthful."

"I haven't any more room," Terri pleaded.

Elena smiled, at her most charming. "To please me," she coaxed.

When she put it like that, she was impossible to resist, and Terri obediently forced the mouthful down. But it was a mistake. Without warning, her stomach rebelled. Quick as a flash, Elena dashed to the bathroom and returned with a towel just in time.

"I'm sorry," Terri choked when the storm had passed.

"It was my fault," Elena said penitently. "Come, I'll help you to the bathroom and find you a change of clothes."

Terri emerged a few minutes later to find Elena changing the bed linen with a clean nightgown laid out. She chivied Terri back into bed. The clean linen felt cool and smelled delicious and Terri snuggled down gratefully, closing her eyes. Elena watched her for a moment with a look on her face that no one had ever seen before. It was a look of protective love and almost incredulous tenderness. It would have lightened Terri's heart if she could have seen it, but she never opened her eyes. After a while, Elena crept out.

Slowly, Terri sank into a fevered sleep and a strange dream came to her. She called it a dream although she had the sensation of awakening and seeing everything that happened. She seemed to split into two people, and her other self rose from the bed and stood looking down at her. She had Terri's face but her manner was different. She was poised and purposeful, with defiant eyes that confronted the world—or any man in it—on equal terms. She had almost nothing in common with the shy, retiring young woman who'd come to Venice so many weeks and so many ages ago.

"Who are you?" Terri whispered.

"I am Teresa."

"No," she protested. "Teresa was *his* name for me. I won't be Teresa."

"You have no choice. This was bound to happen. He said your Italian blood would speak to you, and now it does. It speaks of love and pain, of passion and hate. And when it speaks of the vendetta, it sings. I am Teresa, and I am *you.*"

Then the phantom lay down on the bed and the two of them became one again. At once Terri seemed to fall asleep and when she awoke everything was normal. Her temperature had fallen and she was herself once more.

Except that she was no longer sure who she was. The dream had been real and vivid, and she was de-

termined to understand it. Maurizio was right. She was
Italian by blood, and the love and pain she'd discovered had tapped deep wells of feeling within her that
she'd never dreamed of in her English life. The passion and violence of those feelings had brought her
Italian side alive. The dream had merely crystallized
something that was already happening.

"Vendetta," she murmured. "You were right,
Maurizio. And when you discover how right you were,
you'll wish you'd never brought Teresa to life."

Elena came in, and seeing Terri sitting up and
looking better, the countess beamed. She herself
looked tired and pale but she bustled energetically over
to the bed and laid her hand against Terri's forehead.
"Good," she said. "Your fever has gone and now you
can start to get well."

"I feel bad about you looking after me," Terri said.
"It's not your job."

Elena shrugged. "I like looking after people," she
said simply. "And there's no one else for me to care
for. I've really enjoyed caring for you, dear." She
smiled. "Or must I call you Teresa now?"

"Why—why should you think that?"

"Because while you were asleep you kept saying, 'I
am Teresa. I am Teresa,' over and over. And once you
said, 'This was bound to happen.' Were you having a
bad dream?"

"It was a dream, but I'm not sure it was a bad one,"
Terri said thoughtfully. "It made me understand
something about myself, and now I'm stronger."

"Why did you run away from Maurizio? Was it to
do with what Denise told you about Leo?"

"Yes. Leo fell sick on Terranotte, and Maurizio
kept him there. Even when I came to Venice looking

for him, Maurizio didn't tell me where he was." She took a shuddering breath. "He pretended to love me just so that he could keep tabs on me."

"But why?" Elena asked, bewildered. When Terri didn't answer, she said hesitantly, "Was it connected with Rufio and those things Maurizio said to me at the cemetery?"

"Yes, he thought that you and Leo were—close," Terri said carefully. "When Leo vanished, he thought it would scare you."

If Elena noticed any holes in this carefully edited explanation, she didn't say so. Her only comment was, "Maurizio always made me nervous."

"And you were right."

But then, Elena's volatile nature showed her the bright side. "But at least you found out about Leo," she said. "Where is he now?"

"I don't know. He left the estate and vanished. His mind is wandering. All we know is that he came to Venice. Oh, Elena, I have to find him and I don't know how!"

Elena had gone very pale. "Yes," she whispered. "Yes, we must find him. Poor Leo. That Maurizio is a devil."

"A devil," Terri agreed.

When she was alone again, she found something else that gave her food for thought. Her things had been thoroughly unpacked and put away neatly. The smallest bag had a zipped pocket at the side where she'd packed her passport, but she found the pocket empty. A search revealed the passport neatly stowed away in her bedside drawer, and that made her sit down and think hard.

Without asking outright, there was no way of knowing for sure whether Elena had opened the passport and studied the information it contained, but Elena's frank curiosity and love of gossip were part of her wayward charm, and Terri guessed she hadn't been able to resist the temptation. Which meant that she'd seen the name Mantini and Terri's date of birth. She had enough clues to guess Terri's identity—if she wanted to.

As soon as she was well again, Terri began scouring the city for Leo. She had to search at night as her duties with Elena occupied most of her days. Venice was a small place and she set herself to knock on every door, armed with a picture of Leo. It was tiring, dispiriting work that took her down a thousand dark alleys, up flights of stairs, to confront the puzzled faces of strangers for a brief moment of hope before turning away again, close to despair.

Late one night, she was on the verge of giving up when she decided to try a final building. It had been converted into four tiny apartments that made an L-shape on two sides of a courtyard. As soon as she knocked on one door, lights came on in all the other apartments. The door was opened by a middle-aged woman dressed for bed. Terri made her usual speech and showed her the picture, which the woman studied carefully. Her husband appeared and screwed up his eyes at the picture, but shook his head.

There was a step behind Terri and she moved aside to allow a girl of about sixteen to enter the apartment. From the way the man and woman screamed, *"Maria,"* and pounced on her, firing questions, it was clear that this was the couple's daughter returned from a date with her boyfriend—much too late. Maria looked sheepish but uncowed, and deflected the inquisition by studying the photograph.

"I think I may have seen him," she said slowly.

"You have? When? Where?" Terri asked eagerly.

"Don't you believe her," Maria's mother said with grim humor. "She's hoping we'll forget that she should have been home two hours ago."

A young woman of about twenty emerged from one of the other apartments and strolled toward the little crowd. Maria thrust the picture at her. "Here, Damiata," she said. "Didn't I see you talking to him once?"

Terri held her breath as Damiata took the picture and stared at it. But then she shrugged and shook her head. "I've never seen him," she said.

"Are you sure?" Terri pleaded.

Damiata yawned. "I'm sure. He hasn't been around here."

"But *you* thought you'd seen him," Terri said desperately to Maria.

Maria shrugged and grinned, as if admitting that her interest had been a smoke screen to hide her from her parents' suspicions, and Terri's heart sank again.

People appeared from the other apartments and studied Leo's face but they all shrugged. Terri looked around, hoping to see Damiata again, but she'd vanished. She thanked everyone and went out into the dark street with slow, weary steps.

She froze as she saw the dark shadow of a man standing beneath the lamp. Despite the dim light, she knew the outline, even before he stepped forward and spoke her name in accents that made her heart lurch. "What are you doing here, Maurizio?"

"The same as you. I, too, spend my nights going from door to door. I promised you I would search every corner of Venice."

"I thought you had employees to do your dirty work," she said cruelly.

"I do. I thought they'd find him but they didn't, so now I'm conducting my own search."

"On valuable casino time?" she mocked. "Won't your customers miss you?"

"Let them. This is more important. I gave you my word to find Leo, and I'm going to keep it."

Despite herself, she was touched, but she was Teresa now, not Terri, and Teresa refused to weaken. "If you *can* keep it," she said. "Suppose he's dead?"

She was bitterly gratified to see that that thought hurt him almost as much as it hurt her, and it must have shown in her face because Maurizio winced and said, "You enjoyed saying that, didn't you?"

"Yes. There's a lot of pleasure in paying you back in your own coin. You used to call me Teresa because you were speaking to my Italian side—"

"I told you that one day you would come to know that side of yourself."

"And you were right. I *am* Teresa, and I love being Teresa because she's everything I wasn't, strong and confident, not a deluded little fool who'll believe every lie a man tells her. You won't like her. She's learned the lessons *you* had to teach, about cruelty and deception, how to be cold and hard to people who love you—"

"*No*," he said with soft vehemence. "I was never cold and hard to you. It may have begun that way—before I knew you—it's true that then you were just part of my revenge. But from the first moment we met, you entered my heart, although it took me too long to realize that everything had changed."

"How convenient!" she scoffed. "So you admit you set out to make use of me."

"Only in the beginning—"

"Do you think it's all right to use people as pawns as long as you don't know them? But anything can be done in the sacred name of vendetta, can't it?"

Without waiting for an answer, she turned and began to walk away. He moved quickly to keep up with her. "Teresa, please believe I'm not proud of myself. I've had time for bitter regrets about what I've done to you. If anything has happened to Leo, I shall never forgive myself."

"It's *my* lack of forgiveness that should worry you, Maurizio," she snapped.

"It does. Your hatred weighs on my heart day and night. That and my conscience are burdens almost too great to bear."

"Bear them," she raged. "They're nothing to the burdens you'll bear if my brother's body is fished out of the water."

She moved quickly to get away from him. But his voice stopped her. "Leo isn't dead."

She whirled and stared at him, but her limbs seemed to be frozen. Maurizio came closer. "I don't believe that Leo can be dead," he told her. "If he were, you would know before I did. Your heart would tell you."

"If only I could be sure."

They'd reached a street lamp. Now she had a good look at Maurizio and the sight shocked her. For the first time, she realized that he really suffered. His face was ravaged. He was thinner and there were dark circles under haunted eyes. He looked like a man who seldom slept, and what sleep he did have was tormented by nightmares. But when she thought of her own nightmares, she could feel no pity for him.

"I hope you're right about Leo," she said. "But as time goes on with no sign of him, I get more and more afraid that I'll never see him again. And if that happens, may God forgive you, because I never will."

Abruptly she turned and ran away. A pain had started in her heart and it threatened to overwhelm her. Her love was dead, yet she knew she had to get away from the sight of Maurizio's tormented face while she had the strength.

In a few minutes, she reached the Palazzo Calvani and let herself in quietly. But if she thought to pass unnoticed, she'd reckoned without Elena's watchful eyes. As she reached the upper floor, Elena was already there, in her dressing gown, looking at her watch. "You're so late," she said. "I was getting worried about you."

"I'm sorry. I hope I didn't disturb you."

"I never go to sleep until you come in."

Terri stared. "I didn't know that."

"I listen for the front door, then your footsteps coming up the stairs. They always sound heavy and I know you haven't found Leo. One night I hope to hear them light and happy." She took Terri's hand between hers. "You're like ice. Come and get warm. We don't want you catching cold again."

She drew Terri into her own room, and made her sit down on the huge, luxurious double bed. "Francisco won't disturb us," she said with a shrug. She began to rub Terri's hands. "Obviously you didn't find Leo tonight."

Terri shook her head, too tired and wretched to speak. Elena looked at her suddenly. "But something's happened," she said. Her hand flew to her mouth. "You've had bad news of Leo? Oh, my God! Tell me quickly."

"It's not Leo. It's Maurizio. I met him in the street."

"What did he have to say for himself?"

"What *can* he say? He's searching, too—trying to ease his conscience, if he has such a thing."

"But it upset you to see him, didn't it?" Elena said sympathetically. "Do you still love him so much?"

"I don't love him," Terri said in a hard voice. "And he doesn't love me. He never did. It was nothing but an illusion." Then her grief came welling up, making her cry out, "But it was a lovely illusion. The world is so cold without it. *I want my illusion back.*" Tears streamed down her face and she crossed her arms over herself, rocking back and forth.

"I know how cold the world can be," Elena whispered. "It's only when love is over that you understand what it meant to you." She took Terri's sobbing form in her arms and stroked her hair. "*Cara* Teresa," she said softly, "I'm here. Hold on to me."

Terri hardly heard the words but she reached out blindly, feeling something ease in her heart as she was enfolded in a mother's loving warmth and comfort for the first time in her life. The two women sat like that for a long time.

The smile on Rufio's face was the first thing that greeted Maurizio as he put on the light. It was the same smile as always, fixed, unchanging, serving only as a reminder that he was dead. Maurizio averted his eyes.

After a moment, Bruno came in. "Still no news?" he asked.

Maurizio shook his head. "I've been to every house in Venice," he said heavily. "There's nowhere else to look." Bruno didn't answer and Maurizio turned on him savagely. "He's not dead," he shouted. "You're not to say that."

"But it's not I who says it." Bruno pointed out. "It's your own conscience."

Maurizio stared at him from haunted eyes. His face was that of a man enduring the tortures of the damned. "*She* thinks he's dead," he whispered in horror.

"You saw her tonight? What did she say?"

"She said—" Maurizio shuddered. "She said that God must forgive me, because she never would."

Bruno nodded like a man who knew there was nothing to add. He glanced at Rufio's portrait. "I've been thinking of Rufio, who was so gentle and loving," he said. "I don't believe there was a vengeful bone in his body."

"Shut up!" Maurizio ordered him. *"Shut up."*

He buried his face in his hands.

As Christmas approached, life in the Palazzo Calvani became hectic. Elena was in her element, giving lavish parties and gifts, and buying lots of new clothes. She took Terri along on shopping expeditions and always bought her some costly trinket. She deflected all protests with a dazzling smile and the observation, "It's Christmas." But sometimes she would take Terri's hand between her own two little hands and say gravely, "I want to do this—please," in such a strange tone that Terri would wonder again exactly how much Elena suspected.

Her official Christmas gift to Terri was a long velvet cloak. "For you to wear at Carnival," she said. She chuckled like a delighted child. "Carnival is such fun. I start to prepare for it on the day after Christmas."

Francisco's gift was a pearl necklace, so fine and beautiful that Terri gasped. The pearls were perfectly matched, with a soft glow that spoke of luxury and cost. "I can't accept this," she said quickly.

"But why not?" he asked with a smile.

"It's much too expensive."

"It's the best, and the best is what I wanted to give you to show my gratitude for all you do in this house."

"I don't do anything much..."

"On the contrary. You transform whatever you touch. My mother is happier, Elena is calmer, everything runs smoothly." He carried her hand to his lips. "Thank you, *signorina,* for the way you've transformed my home."

Once the gesture would have embarrassed her, but she'd left that gaucherie behind her, and now she was sufficiently poised to smile and let Francisco finish, without showing how much she disliked his touch.

After such generosity by her employers, she was embarrassed by the comparative modesty of her gifts to them. For Francisco she bought a silver pen, little enough amidst the luxury he took for granted, but it blew a hole in her budget. She was careful to give it to him in Elena's presence and he smiled and thanked her formally. But later he found her alone and said, "I must thank you again for your gift. It was charming of you to be so observant."

"Observant?"

"You noticed that I'd lost my other pen. Elena gave it to me and I'd had it for years. But now I have yours, which I will treasure."

In fact she hadn't noticed that his pen had disappeared. She'd picked the present at random. "Perhaps I should have chosen something else," she said. "I'm sure Elena will wish to replace her gift to you herself."

He gave his quiet laugh. "She hasn't even noticed that it's gone. How different from you, Teresa, who notices everything about me."

"Please, you're reading too much into it."

"Am I? I hope not. Haven't you noticed how well we understand each other?"

"No," she said, determined to put an end to this conversation. "I can't say I have. Will you excuse me now, please?"

She hurried away without looking back, so she never saw the satisfied smile with which he looked after her or the way he nodded his head.

She chose Elena's present with great care, her first gift to her true mother. It seemed to her that Elena had every material luxury that money could buy, but nobody with whom to share her interests. One evening recently, the talk had somehow strayed to archaeology and Elena had revealed an avid interest in the subject. Terri had been only slightly surprised. Elena was knowledgeable about art, and from art to archaeology was a short step. So Terri purchased a lavishly illustrated set of reference works and was rewarded by seeing Elena's face light up. "I'd been thinking of buying these for myself," she cried ecstatically. "How did you know?"

"I remembered what we were discussing a few weeks ago," Terri reminded her, laughing. "You talked about digs and old bones and your eyes were shining."

"And you remembered that?" Elena's face softened. "How kind you are. This is the best gift of all."

"Better than your diamonds?" Terri couldn't resist asking, for Francisco's gift to his wife had been a diamond set of such magnificence that all Venice was talking about them.

Elena shrugged. "They'll go into the bank vault and I'll never see them. He gives me jewels every year. They're a good investment." Her eyes grew suddenly faraway. "It's strange. I used to think it would be wonderful to be showered with diamonds. But in those days, I never knew...so many things..." She checked herself, and after a pause continued. "I never knew how much better it was to have a present like this, that someone had really thought about."

There were tears in her eyes and the next moment Terri was enveloped in a scented embrace that went on for a long time. She hugged Elena, feeling the tears prick her eyelids, too.

There was one other present that she told nobody about. She scoured the shops of Venice until she found a silk tie with a really outrageous pattern. Only a very young man could have worn such a tie and held up his head. Having bought it, she laid it quietly away in her drawer, promising herself that she would one day give it to Leo.

Chapter Eleven

"*Early this morning, the body of a young man was taken from the Grand Canal. His identity is unknown and he is being kept at the public mortuary in the hope that...*"

Terri was helping to arrange flowers for the New Year's Eve ball at the palazzo that evening when the voice on the radio made her stiffen with shock. Cold tremors went through her and her hand tightened convulsively on a vase. When she could move again, she rushed into the hall and put on her coat.

Elena appeared as she was ready to go. "*Cara,* whatever is the matter?" she said as soon as she saw Terri's face.

"They've taken a dead man from the water," Terri said. "I'm going to the mortuary now."

Elena's hands flew to her pale face. "Oh, no," she said piteously. "It mustn't be Leo. It *can't* be."

Francisco looked out into the hall. "Elena," he called peremptorily. "There's still much to do."

"One moment," she called back. "Oh, Teresa, if only I could come with you—"

"No, it would look strange. I'll call you as soon as I know." Impulsively, Terri kissed Elena's cheek before hurrying away.

A chill hush hung over Venice. The dark water lay sullen and undisturbed. As Terri walked through the thick snow in the twilight, she tried not to think of what lay on that mortuary slab. It need not be Leo. It could be anybody. But her heart was breaking as though it knew that all hope would soon be dead.

At the mortuary she was given a form to fill out, then a white-coated attendant led her into a quiet room. The body was laid out, covered by a sheet, and it took all her courage to approach it. After an anxious glance at her, the attendant revealed the face. She gasped with shock and clutched the slab to stop herself falling.

It wasn't Leo.

She felt a pair of strong arms steadying her, helping her to walk from the room. The attendant said, "This often happens. We have a room where people can recover. This way."

She clung to her rescuer until she was sitting in a leather chair. A familiar voice said, "Steady now. Close your eyes for a moment."

"Maurizio."

He sat quickly beside her. "I heard it on the radio," he said. "Like you I rushed here, fearing the worst, but thank God! *Thank God.*"

He, too, was shaking. Moved by blind instinct, Terri put out her arms and they clung together. For a moment, enmity was forgotten in their mutual, desperate need for comfort. "I was so afraid," she said in a choked voice. "I was sure it would be Leo—I couldn't bear to see him—but I had to—"

"Do you think I don't know how you feel? In the time it took to walk here, I was in hell." They held each other more tightly, bonded by their shared experience. "Teresa," he murmured, "Teresa, it wasn't him. Leo is still alive somewhere."

"But *where?*"

"I don't know but he's *still alive*. We must both hold on to that."

At last she drew back and brushed a hand over her face. "I've got to call Elena," she said. "I promised to let her know at once."

"There's a phone just outside in the hall."

He went with her. Terri thought she was in command of herself, but as soon as she reached out for the receiver, her hand began to shake uncontrollably. Maurizio didn't speak but he quietly dialed the number of the palazzo and waited, listening to the ringing. When it was answered, he handed Terri the receiver and moved away.

"Elena," Terri said huskily, "it wasn't Leo. Truly, there's no mistake. It was nothing like him." Maurizio didn't look around but his stillness was eloquent as Terri fell silent to listen. "Don't cry," she said at last. "I'll be home soon. It's all right."

She hung up and leaned against the wall, drained of energy. Maurizio took her arm and led her outside. Darkness had fallen and a thick mist turned the city to shadows. Without saying a word, he guided her into a café and toward a seat. He returned from the bar with two brandies. "How was she?"

"Relieved. She couldn't stop crying."

"Over Leo?" he asked in a neutral voice. "A young man she barely knows?" Terri glanced at him but didn't say anything. "How much of the truth does she guess, do you think?"

She sighed. "I've no idea. Sometimes I think she knows in her heart that we're her children but she's too nervous to say anything. If it gets out—" She shrugged.

"It could be a disaster for her," he said. To her relief, he spoke without his usual cutting irony. He saw Terri looking at him and said quickly, "I'm not planning to tell Francisco. After everything that's happened, revenge doesn't seem so important now."

Terri gave a wan smile. "How sad that you waited this long to learn that."

"Yes," he said heavily.

It was strange to Terri to be sitting here with Maurizio with no buzz between them. At one time the air had sung, first with love, then with hate. Now there was only calm and weariness, as though they'd fought each other to a standstill. There was even a strange comfort in his presence. He was the only person in the world who understood what she'd been through in the last hour, because he'd been through it, too. She'd seen him passionate, tender, ironic and bitter. But now he was kind, and that was the most painful thing of all, because it tormented her with a vision of what might have been.

"You look worn-out," he said.

"I was up half the night helping with preparations for the party."

"How do you keep going, with this on your mind?"

She gave a brief, mirthless laugh. "The same way that you do, I suppose. It's always there, every moment, night and day."

"Like a fiend laying in wait when you awaken and haunting you when you try to sleep," Maurizio agreed.

"Yes, it's exactly like that."

He was shocked at her pallor and the dark shadows beneath her eyes. She'd lost weight. He could see it in her face, and he'd felt it when he'd held her in the mortuary. The thought of her body made him ache, but not with desire; rather, it was a kind of anguished pity at her suffering. He remembered how she'd looked as she lay naked in his arms, how softly rounded her limbs had been, how he'd rejoiced at her beauty. It was harder to see physical beauty in this thin, tormented woman, yet her hold on his heart had grown stronger. If only he had her in his bed now, how tenderly he would embrace her, soothing her with caresses until she fell asleep safely in his arms. If only she would let him, he would spend his life trying to drive the sadness from her face, and ask nothing in return but to know that she was his.

Suddenly, she met his eyes, and for a searing moment all barriers were down between them. They looked into each other's defenselessness, and it was unbearable. "Teresa," he whispered.

"No—no." She began to cry in a quiet, despairing way that tore him apart.

He seized her hands across the table. "Please, don't cry," he said urgently.

"I'm so tired," she said softly.

He didn't have to ask what she meant. Waiting and hoping had left him almost at the end of his strength, as well. But what little he had left was at her service. "I'll do anything," he said.

"But there's nothing you *can* do, nothing either of us can do but wait, maybe forever."

"No," he said desperately. "This can't go on forever."

"But it can. I'm beginning to think we'll never discover the truth, and if we don't—"

He laid a hand across her mouth. "Don't say it," he pleaded. "There are some truths too terrible to face."

"But we've both faced this one already, haven't we?"

"Until I restore Leo to you, there can never be love between us," he said heavily. "Suppose I can *never* restore him to you?"

She looked him in the eyes. "Did you forgive Elena for *your* brother's death?" she asked. He winced and closed his eyes, shaking his head. She was silent. There was nothing left to say. "I'd better go now," she said. "There's still a lot to do for tonight. For you, too, I expect."

"Oh, yes," he agreed without enthusiasm. "We're all going to have a wonderful time at the Midas. I'll walk you back."

"There's no need. I know my way like a Venetian now."

"Let me stay with you as long as I can."

He walked beside her until they'd almost reached the palazzo. At the last corner, he stopped and held her so that her head rested on his shoulder. "It could have been so different," he said huskily.

She put her arms about his body. "Yes," she said. "It could have been different. If only we'd met some other way."

"Can't we—?"

"Not until Leo is safe. Perhaps never. That's the truth and I can't change it, however much I wa—" She stopped.

"However much we want to. I didn't know until this moment what we might have had."

"Nor I. But we have to forget it."

"We can never forget it," he said somberly. "It may torment us all our lives but neither of us will ever know the peace of forgetting what we've learned today. There's no peace in love. Why should there be?"

He tilted her chin and laid his lips gently against hers. It was a kiss without passion, a kiss of love and comfort, tender and self-forgetful, and it broke her heart. "We'll never forget," he murmured.

"We'll never forget," she agreed. "But when I pass out of your sight around that corner, I'm your enemy again, Maurizio."

He didn't try to protest. He knew it had to be. Gently he released her and watched as she walked to the corner. There she looked back. "I never asked," she said. "How did your brother die?"

"He drowned himself. I reclaimed his body from the mortuary."

"Then today was doubly terrible for you. I'm so sorry. Goodbye, Maurizio. Goodbye."

He strained his eyes to see where she'd been standing. Then the mist cleared for a moment and he saw that she was gone. All he could hear was the water lapping softly against the stones, and her final "Goodbye" floating back to him like a whisper from the shadows.

The mist lifted during the evening and the Grand Canal was brilliant as midnight approached on the last night of the year. From every palace, light flooded out, and music and merrymaking could be heard along the water. At the Midas and the Palazzo Calvani, fresh bottles of champagne were broken open as the hands of the clock approached twelve.

Bruno, capering by with a young woman, studied Maurizio with disapproval. "You're sober, nephew."

"Unfortunately, yes." The clock struck one and he forced a smile to his face, raising his voice. "It's nearly midnight. Make your wishes for the new year." The clock struck two and he seized a champagne bottle to refill the glasses of those around him.

A woman planted a kiss on Maurizio's mouth. "We all wish for love, of course," she cried. "What else is there to wish for?"

"What else?" Maurizio echoed mechanically.

Three. Four.

"Tell us who you're thinking of," she sang out.

Five. Six.

"I keep my heart safe so that I can give a little piece of it to every woman," he told her charmingly.

Seven. Eight.

"Maurizio, darling, you always have just the right answer."

Nine. Ten.

"More champagne!"

Eleven.

"It's nearly midnight."

"Happy New Year, everyone!"

"Happy New—"

"This year's going to be *wonderful*."

Twelve.

The room erupted in cheering and singing. Multi-colored streamers poured down. Corks popped.

"Happy New Year, nephew."

"Happy New Year, Uncle."

Maurizio turned away to the window, wondering how much more jollity he could endure. The Grand Canal was alive with revelers. He looked past them to where the curve hid the Palazzo Calvani. She was there and she was thinking of him. He knew that without a doubt.

How can I ask forgiveness, when I have none to give? he thought bitterly. *There's no forgiveness for me in heaven or on earth. But yet—forgive me, Teresa, for the wrong I've done!*

The snow lasted three weeks, then vanished overnight as the weather turned warmer. Suddenly, everyone was talking about the carnival that would take place at the end of February. Elena explained that the name came from the Latin words *carne* meaning the flesh, and *vale* meaning farewell.

"It's the last thing that happens before Lent when we must all renounce the pleasures of the flesh and be very, very good," she pouted. "So, before Lent begins, we have several days to enjoy the worldly things. Oh, *cara* you should see the streets of Venice during Carnival, full of people in fancy costumes. And there are lots of lovely parties when we eat and drink as much as we like, and—other pleasures." She finished on a chuckle.

The young man in the morgue had been identified and there were no further scares. But as the weeks went by, neither was there any news of Leo, and Terri's heart hardened again toward Maurizio. Their brief moment of tenderness and understanding remained only as a memory that tormented her, not as a hope for the future.

Elena plunged into an orgy of planning entertainments and buying clothes. She had two Columbine costumes made for herself and Terri, each with a tight satin bodice and a huge frothy white skirt made of tulle, decorated with glitter. The two costumes were identical in every respect except that the glitter was gold on one and silver on the other.

When they tried them on and surveyed themselves side by side in the mirror, Terri drew in her breath. They were the same height and size, the same coloring, and with their masks on, they might have been twins. Surely Elena would see . . . ?

"Perfetto," the *contessa* declared.

"Elena—"

"Oh, please don't say again that I give you too much," Elena begged. "I love to give you things. I used to think—perhaps I might have a daughter one day. How I would love to take her shopping, and talk to her about things I can't tell anyone else." She hesitated before saying with a little sigh, "I hope she would have been like you. Please let me spoil you, *cara*. I do so long for someone to spoil."

She put her head to one side with a mixture of pleading and coaxing, and Terri's heart turned over. If only they could have known each other before. "I must admit, I rather enjoy being spoiled," she said.

Elena didn't look directly as Terri as she asked, "What about your mother? Didn't she ever spoil you?"

Terri answered equally casually, "I never knew my real mother. Madge, my adoptive mother—well, we just never managed to love each other. She did her duty by me."

"Poor Terri. How dreary to be done duty by." She hesitated before asking casually, "Did you ever want to go and find your real mother?"

Terri took a deep breath. Perhaps this was the chance to tell Elena the truth. Yet even now, some cautious instinct warned her not to blurt everything out at once. Elena's words had invited her on, but only a little way. "I've thought about it," she said, choosing her words with care. "But she's got her own life without me. She might be married—and perhaps—perhaps her husband isn't a very nice man. I'd like to know her—but I don't want to do her any harm."

In the long silence that followed, Terri's heart beat so loudly that she was sure Elena must be able to hear it. At last, the countess said softly, "Whoever she is, I think she's very lucky to have so kind and thoughtful a daughter. You think of her and her difficulties, that perhaps she has a husband who knows nothing of her past and who would take terrible revenge on her if he were to find out." She clasped her hands together and Terri saw how thin and nervous they were beneath the rings that flashed and sparkled on them. "But also, perhaps—she has never forgotten her children—her child. Perhaps she has more of a mother's heart than she realized all those years ago, and her loss has torn at her ever since, and if only she had more courage—" She broke off with a little gasp and for a moment her eyes were suspiciously bright. In another moment she would have taken her mother in her arms, pleading for her recognition, and her love.

But with one of her swift changes of mood Elena recovered herself and glanced at the mirror with its giveaway twin reflection. "On second thought," she said, "I don't think I like these costumes, after all."

"But you've bought them now."

"So? The shop can resell them. Take it off, *cara*. We'll wear something else."

Terri let her breath out slowly, trying to steady herself against disappointment. Briefly Elena had opened a door through which Terri could glimpse their future relationship; one of honesty and love. But at the last moment Elena's courage had failed her and she'd hurried to close the door again. Terri couldn't reveal the truth now. Nor could she tell when the chance might come again.

The party at the Palazzo Calvani was *the* event of the carnival. Everyone who was anyone was there. The champagne was the finest, the jewels the most glittering, the costumes the most outrageous. The Calvanis wore eighteenth-century costumes of black and silver. Terri's costume was also eighteenth century, but everything was snowy white, from the gleaming satin brocade of the hooped skirt to the lace ruffles. Terri had fallen in love with it. The depth of the square neckline had given her qualms, as she'd never before worn anything that revealed so much of her bosom, but Elena's was just as low, and she soon suppressed her modesty. The final touch was the shining white wig with hair piled high on her head and one long ringlet brushing her shoulder.

When Francisco saw her, he said, "Tonight you must wear the pearls I gave you for Christmas. They're perfect with that costume."

This was so obviously true that Terri could find no way to refuse, although she managed to dodge his attempt to fasten the necklace around her neck.

They were in Elena's bedroom where Terri had gone to put the final touches to her appearance. This was Elena's idea so that her own maid could tend the two of them. When Francisco had departed, Elena dismissed the maid and said quietly, "There's a very strange story going around Venice, about Maurizio."

"What do they say about him?" Terri asked, trying to sound indifferent.

"That he's going mad. He went into a café for a snack, took out a forty-thousand-lire note and sat staring at it. The bill was thirty-five thousand, but when Giovanni, the proprietor, asked for it, Maurizio said he'd pay by check because he didn't have any money on him. Giovanni reminded him of the note he'd been holding, but Maurizio insisted he was mistaken. Apparently, he got terribly angry, gave Giovanni a check for twice the amount and stormed out. Giovanni says he's going to frame the check to prove that he's the first man in Venice who ever got an extra lira out of Maurizio. Did you ever hear such an odd story?"

"Perhaps he's been affected by the spirit of Carnival," Terri suggested lightly. But she was sure she knew what had made Maurizio behave so strangely. The note must have been the one she'd given him as a tip at their first meeting, and nothing would make him part with it. It was practically a declaration of love, and for a moment her heart was full of pain. But she suppressed it. That was weakness. She'd yielded to weakness once, but not again. Not until Leo was found.

The guests began to arrive at nine o'clock and soon the room was awash with glamorous and outlandish costumes. Terri began by keeping close to Elena in case the countess needed her, but Elena soon waved her away, ordering her to enjoy herself. When the dancing began, Terri was much in demand, and for three hours she gave herself up to flirting and laughing and appearing to have a wonderful time.

At last she made her way to the window to escape the crush and took a glass of champagne from a passing waiter. As she stood sipping it and fanning herself, a crowd of revelers surged along the street below the window. Looking down, she saw a riot of colorful costumes, Harlequins and Columbines, Pantalones and Pulcinellas, clowns and devils. Then they passed and the alley was quiet again.

But not quite empty. A solitary Harlequin figure stood beneath a lamp, leaning against the wall. In his hand he held something that glittered. His slim body was covered with a skin-hugging costume of multicolored diamonds. On his head he wore a black tricorne and a black mask covered the upper part of his face. At first sight, he looked exactly like a thousand others who'd thronged the city for the last few days. And yet, there was something different about him, something familiar about the way he was standing, something that made Terri's heart pound.

"Leo," she breathed softly.

She opened the window and leaned out, making the Harlequin glance up. Terri strained to see the shape of his mouth but the light was too poor. All she could tell was that the sight of her had made him grow very still. She didn't speak, fearful of alarming him, but for a long silent moment their eyes met, and all the while her conviction grew.

At last she ventured to say, "Why are you alone, Harlequin? No one should be alone for Carnival." He put his head on one side, considering, but he didn't answer. If only he would speak, she thought. Then she would know by the sound of his voice. "Why don't you come up?" she asked lightly. "Perhaps your Columbine is here?"

He considered again, then nodded. "I'll come down and let you in," she said.

Swiftly she closed the window and made her way through the crowd. Her heels tapped out a pattern as she sped down the marble staircase to the side door and pulled it open. Her heart was beating with joyful anticipation.

But there was no one there.

She ran to the end of the alley but there was no sign of him in the rabbit warren of streets. Desperately she retraced her steps and hurried to the other end but he was gone. There was only the night and the soft lapping of the dark water. She almost cried aloud in her bitter disappointment.

Then something caught her eye. On the ground where Harlequin had stood, there now lay the glittering object he'd been holding. Terri picked it up and saw that it was a small gilt replica of a winged lion, the symbol of Venice. "A lion," she breathed in English. Then something impelled her to repeat it in Italian. *"Leone...Leo..."*

It might be no more than coincidence but she didn't think so. The love and comradeship of years spoke and told her that her brother had been here, reaching out

to her and then running away. Why? What—*who*—
was he afraid of?

There'd been false hopes before but this time her
spirit was up and she was determined to do something. She ran back inside, spoke hurriedly to one of
the servants, then hurried upstairs for her velvet cloak.
It was time she confronted Maurizio again, and this
time, she promised herself, it would be no sentimen-
tal interlude, letting him off the hook, but a challenge
that he couldn't avoid.

Francisco stood in the middle of the hall and
watched her disappear upstairs. When she was out of
sight, he summoned the servant Terri had spoken to.
"What did the *signorina* say?" he demanded.

"She told me to send for the boatman, Excellency."

"Did she say where she was going?"

"Yes, Excellency. To the Midas Hotel."

"Very well. Be about your business. *I* will deliver
the message."

Arriving at the landing stage a few moments later,
Terri found the motorboat ready, its engine humming. But when the boatman reached up to help her
in, she drew back with a little gasp. "I heard you were
going to the Midas," Francisco said, "and since I'm
going there myself, I decided to act as your boatman—unless, of course, you have some objection."

It was impossible to object, so Terri make the appropriate response, but actually she was dismayed.
Francisco knew nothing about Maurizio's conceal-
ment of Leo or the real cause of her quarrel with him,
and he mustn't suspect the truth, for Elena's sake.
Unless she could shake him off when they reached the

Midas, it would be impossible to speak frankly to Maurizio.

Suddenly, a thought struck her and her hand flew to her mouth. "Oh, dear!"

Francisco glanced briefly aside from steering the boat. "What's the matter?"

"I'm supposed to be helping Elena with the party, and I just walked out without saying anything to her. How rude of me!"

Francisco grinned. "To tell the truth, I slipped away secretly myself. But it's most unlike you. Usually you're quite frighteningly conscientious, and very, very English. Tonight you've behaved like an Italian, acting on impulse. What was the impulse, I wonder? A lover?"

"I have no lover," Terri said firmly.

"Not even Maurizio?" Francisco asked idly. He seemed to be concentrating on the water.

"Least of all Maurizio."

"Then he's not the reason you're going to the Midas? Forgive me if I seem inquisitive. Since you're living in my home, I naturally feel a fatherly interest in your welfare."

"It's perfectly all right," Terri said. "It's true I'm going to see Maurizio. I have things to say to him. But they're not words of love."

"I'm glad. I've told you I respect him because he's ruthless and formidable, but he's not a good man for a young woman to become involved with."

"Don't worry about me," she said grimly. "My heart is armored."

The Midas was dazzling against the night. Another moment and they were at the landing stage, climbing the steps into the casino. She saw Maurizio as soon as she entered the roulette room. He was moving from table to table, exchanging pleasantries with the gamblers. Here, too, there were Harlequins and Columbines, and clowns of all kinds. Maurizio himself was dressed as usual in white dinner jacket, and in the garish crowd he stood out by his quiet presence and authority. Pain seized Terri's heart. She'd seen him so often like this before, and loved him. Now she must crush love, but her heart refused to still its beating, almost as if it didn't know he was an enemy.

An attendant was waiting to take her cloak. She unclasped it and in the same moment Francisco stepped forward, laid his hands over hers and lifted the cloak away. It was unnecessary but she smiled a polite thanks just the same, trying not to flinch as his fingers briefly brushed against her neck.

Maurizio was deadly still, watching her. His eyes burned as they gazed, letting her know more clearly than words ever could that he was on the rack. Terri faced him with her head up, her eyes sparkling with defiance. Francisco observed them both, a chill smile on his face. "There are two places free at this table," he murmured, leaning close to her. "Unless there's another game you would rather play."

"Roulette will do splendidly, thank you," she said, following him to the table and letting him draw out a chair for her. The gorgeous dress splayed out in a froth of white satin as she sat down. A pile of chips appeared in front of her.

"I took the liberty of ordering them for you and having them put on my own account," Francisco explained.

"Thank you," she said crisply. At any other time she would have refused to be in his debt, but tonight the knowledge of Maurizio's disapproving eyes on her was like heady wine. She took a pile of chips and played them. For a moment, the impulse that had brought her here was forgotten in the bitter pleasure of knowing that he was on hot coals. Let him suffer as he'd made her suffer.

The wheel spun and in moments her chips were gone. She played the rest and they vanished, too. More chips appeared at her elbow. She staked them defiantly, and just as defiantly watched them vanish. Maurizio was looking at her, not moving, his mouth tense.

When all her chips were gone, she laughed and said, "It's not my lucky night."

"Don't forget the saying," Francisco murmured. "Lucky in love, unlucky at chance. Who knows where your lucky love is waiting?"

Terri gave a slight shrug of her shoulders. "I don't think it matters if one is lucky in love," she said coolly. "After all, what *is* love but another game of chance? If one loses, there's always another table and higher stakes." The men around the table were all watching her. At this remark, some of them grinned and edged closer, as if recognizing a new player in the cynical game that Venice had played for centuries. Maurizio didn't move, but it was as though his stillness dominated the room.

"You're right, of course" Francisco said silkily. "But the night is young, and you're here to enjoy yourself. Do you know, *cara,* now I see you in that dress, I know I bought you the right gift. Those pearls look so perfect with white satin. I was inspired."

A small frisson of interest ran around the table, for there wasn't one person there who couldn't estimate the value of the flawless pearls. Still Maurizio didn't move, but there was something terrible in his stillness.

"Your taste is impeccable, Count," Terri said politely.

"It is, *signorina*—" he lifted her hand and kissed it "—in all things."

Francisco released Terri's hand and reached out to sign for more chips but at that moment Maurizio seemed to awaken out of the trance that had held him frozen. He made a gesture to the steward holding out the chit to Francisco and said curtly, "The count and Signorina Wainright are my guests tonight. Their play is on the house. Give me any chits that the count has already signed." The steward did so and Maurizio tore them into tiny pieces. Then he left the room without looking at Terri.

At the bar he ordered a double whiskey and downed it in a single gulp. He was on the verge of ordering another but he stopped himself. To drink more would be an admission that he was losing control, and that was unthinkable. Only he knew how dangerously close to being caught off guard he'd been when Terri had entered the casino tonight. At first his lonely heart had given a leap of gladness. He was still infused by the tenderness of their last meeting. He hadn't seen or heard from her since, but she lived in his mind as she'd been then, gentle, sad, reaching out to him for help. His body remembered her, not as she'd been in their moments of passion, but the way she'd rested her head on his shoulder, and it craved to hold her again in loving kindness.

When she'd walked in, his first thought had been that she'd returned to him. He'd known an almost uncontrollable instinct to go to her, open armed. He would be glad until his dying day that he'd resisted it, for the next moment he'd seen Francisco just behind her, and the byplay with the cloak. Suddenly, he'd noticed the air of sensual sophistication that she wore like an aura, so different from when he'd first known and loved her.

Loved. He could use the word now that she was lost to him. He'd loved her sweetness and simplicity even while he refused to recognize them. And by the time he understood the truth, it was too late. His betrayal had destroyed the very things in her that had touched his heart. Now she looked cool and worldly, a woman who could breathe the corrupt Calvani air and thrive on it, who could accept a fortune in pearls from the most debauched man in Venice, and flaunt them in the face of the man who loved her. Maurizio's head swam with the thought.

"Shall I refill your glass, *signore?*" The barman had the whiskey bottle ready.

"Yes," Maurizio said harshly. *"Yes."*

He was emptying the glass when he saw her reflected behind him in the bar mirror. She was wearing a silver mask through which he could see her eyes watching him intently. He turned slowly to look at her. "Why are you here?" he demanded.

"I want to talk to you, Maurizio. But not here. In private. Your office will do."

He noted the touch of arrogance in her manner, and it dismayed him. He didn't know how to deal with her.

When the door of his office had closed behind them, he indicated her mask, saying, "I wish you'd take that off."

"I think it's very appropriate. From the day we met, you were wearing a mask. You hid behind it while you appraised me for your purposes."

"Take it off," he said through clenched teeth. "I don't know you like that."

"You never knew me. But that's not important now. I came to tell you that I saw Leo tonight."

"When?" he demanded sharply. "Where?"

"Outside the Palazzo Calvani. He was dressed as a Harlequin."

"Did you speak to him?"

"I tried but he vanished."

"How can you be sure it was him? Did you see his face?"

"He wore a black mask and his hair was covered, but it was Leo. He had a winged lion in his hands, which he left behind. *Leone*—Leo. It was him. I know it was."

His shoulders sagged and despair ran through him like icy water. "You can't be sure of that. Why should he run away from you?"

"Perhaps he didn't know me. Who knows what's going on in his mind? The only thing I'm sure of is that he's frightened. What's he scared of, Maurizio?"

"Why do you ask me that?"

"Because you're the man he first ran away from. You kept him prisoner—"

"That's not true. He was ill—he had the best of care."

"Oh, yes, the best of care from a man who needed him alive for his own purposes. I think Leo knew that. I think that through the haze of fever and confusion, he saw clearly the most important thing about you—

that you're cold and heartless, and nothing matters to you but your own purpose. *Nothing.* So he ran away. He didn't know who he was or what you were using him for, but he knew he had to escape. Even in Venice, he tries to approach me but at the last moment he remembers *you,* and becomes afraid. Why, Maurizio? What is he afraid of?"

"This is fantasy," he said, speaking desperately because her voice was like the voice of his own conscience. "You see everything through a distorting mirror. You call me cold and heartless. You must have forgotten a great deal to say that, Teresa."

"I've forgotten nothing," she said, coming closer to him and regarding him from behind the silver mask. "Nothing, do you hear? But I remember it in my own way."

"And the last time we met, in the mortuary on New Year's Eve, when we spoke without hate and walked together, and held each other for comfort—how do you remember that?"

"As an aberration," she said after a tense moment. "As a betrayal of Leo. While he's lost, I had no right to speak to you without hate. I told you that when we parted, we'd be enemies again."

"I'll never be your enemy."

"But you were my enemy from the moment I arrived, Maurizio. You just forgot to tell me about it."

"Is that really why you came here tonight, Teresa? To prove your enmity? To let me see you wearing pearls that he gave you?"

"These?" She touched the necklace. "These are nothing."

"Nothing? You accept a gift worth a king's ransom from your mother's husband and you say it's nothing?"

"Nonsense. I know they're expensive, but to talk about a king's ransom is ridiculous."

"I saw that very necklace on sale for the equivalent of fifty thousand English pounds," he said flatly.

She gasped. "I don't believe it."

"Francisco is a man who pays high for what he wants. If he's set his heart on you, you'd best beware."

Her face flamed at the thought. "That's a disgusting thing to say."

"Is it? You're the one who insists on living under the same roof with him."

"Who introduced me to him, Maurizio?"

"In another world," he said desperately. "When I was another man."

"Just who were you? Who are you now? The man I thought you were didn't exist. *You* don't exist, not really—"

The last word was cut off. Driven beyond endurance, Maurizio had hurled his tumbler so that it smashed against the wall. He seized her shoulders, pulled her around to face him and tore off the necklace, tossing it aside. Then his hands were hard on her bare skin, pulling her close against him so that she was forced to look up into his glittering eyes. "You can't dismiss me so easily," he growled. "Who holds you this minute if I don't exist? Whose heart beats against yours? Who is *this?*"

On the last word he crushed her mouth with his own. She'd known it was going to happen, had told herself she was ready, but the feel of his lips still came as a shock. She tried to pull away but he held her against him while his lips moved over hers. There was both purpose and seduction in those movements, as though he was trying to remind her of what had once been between them and also trying to take her back to the days when he had dominated her for his own ends. But those days were gone. She wrenched herself free.

"Stay away from me," she gasped. "That's over, Maurizio. Over forever."

"It'll never be over as long as we're alive," he said harshly. "What's between us can't be denied. Why do you try?"

"Perhaps because there's nothing between you," came a freezing voice from the doorway.

Shocked, they both looked up to see Francisco standing there, a sardonic expression on his face. His eyes kindling, he moved quickly forward to put himself between them. "My apologies," he said to Terri. "If I hadn't neglected you, you'd never have gone aside with this man."

"Get out of here," Maurizio ordered him savagely.

Francisco ignored him and offered his arm to Terri. "Come, *cara,*" he said. "Let me escort you from this place, and I promise that you'll never be troubled by this ruffian again."

Her head still swimming, Terri missed the nuances of his attitude. She only knew that every inch of her was ablaze with awareness of Maurizio, that Maurizio was her enemy and that she must escape from danger.

"Why, you've lost your pearls, *cara,*" Francisco exclaimed, lifting the necklace from the floor where Maurizio had tossed it. "How careless of you. Let me put this back on."

Too dazed to think clearly, Terri turned slightly so that he could fix the pearls about her neck. She could feel the air vibrating from Maurizio's tension. "Thank you," she said when the clasp was secured.

"And your cloak. I've brought it with me. I'll put it about your shoulders. There."

"Teresa." Maurizio's voice was full of bitter agony. "Why are you doing this to me?"

She just had the strength to look back and meet his eyes. *"Per vendetta,"* she said softly, and saw him go deathly pale as she left the room on Francisco's arm.

Chapter Twelve

The three days and nights of revelry were drawing to a close. On the last night of Carnival, there was scarcely an occupied house left in Venice. All the city tumbled out of doors to join the *festa* in St. Mark's Square.

Terri leaned from Elena's window to watch the boats on the Grand Canal, and listen to the sound of singing and laughter that drifted up from them. Although it was still February, the night was unseasonably mild and most of the revelers stood out in the open so that as the boats passed, the costumes caught the lights, making the spangles throw off a multicolored glitter.

Everywhere, Terri saw outlandish masks, either worn or painted on. There were pale deathlike faces, features covered in spangles, Punchinello masks with long noses, clown faces that wept or laughed and sometimes both. Now and then, Terri noticed the traditional Venetian *baùtta*. This was a voluminous black cloak that enveloped the figure from neck to floor. Over it was a half cape that came down to the elbows. The hat was a black tricorne from the inner rim of which fell a curtain of material that covered the head all around, except for the face, which was hidden by a white mask. The effect was all-concealing and sinister.

Elena had bought an extravagant costume of gold. She sat regarding herself in the mirror as her maid applied the finishing touches to the countess's makeup, but occasionally Elena glanced at Terri and made a face of disappointment. "I wish you'd let me buy you a new dress," she mourned.

"I'm not letting you buy me another thing," Terri declared, turning in from the window. She wanted nothing more. She'd grown increasingly convinced that Elena knew the truth, and her heart longed for her mother to acknowledge her, not publicly but in private. She'd gone out of her way to reassure Elena that she didn't want to harm her, yet there was no response, and inwardly she'd withdrawn a little. She would accept no more gifts if Elena felt unable to give the only one that mattered.

Tonight she had on the white eighteenth-century dress that she'd worn to confront Maurizio at the casino, but she'd left off the wig in favor of her own natural hair. About her neck she wore the pendant that Leo had given her. She no longer had Francisco's pearls. She'd packed them up in their original box and given them to his valet to return to him.

Elena closed her eyes while the maid dusted her with powder. *"Perfetto,"* she declared at last. Then she gave a little scream. "Oh, but look how everything is covered in powder." She pointed to an art book that was lodged casually on the edge of her dressing table and which had received a liberal dusting of powder. Terri brushed the green-and-gold leather cover with her handkerchief. The Calvani crest on the spine proclaimed that it had come from the ancient library downstairs. "Francisco will be so cross," Elena said worriedly. "He hates me to bring books in here. He says I don't take proper care of them."

"How could he think that?" Terri asked mischievously, and the two women laughed together.

"*Cara,* will you—?" Elena held out her hands in plea.

"I'll take it back right now, before anything else happens to it," Terri said.

"It goes at the far end, just behind the desk." Elena looked at the leather cover, whose cracks still bore traces of powder that nothing could remove. "Make sure you put it right back between the other books," she said conspiratorially.

Terri grinned. "Don't worry. There'll be nothing to give you away."

She hurried down the stairs to the huge room at the back of the palace that housed the Calvani book collection and the family archives. It was dark and silent as she gently pushed open the door and fumbled with the bank of switches. At last she found the one that cast a glow over the far end, and went to find the shelf.

She could see the empty space just above her head and climbed up the small ladder to push aside the glass panel. But it wouldn't move. "Damn!" she muttered. "It's locked."

Descending quickly, she began to hunt around the desk for the keys, but there was no sign of them. She hesitated before searching further; she knew that

Francisco often used this desk to work, and was unwilling to pry. But thinking of Elena, she plunged on, pulling open drawers, flicking through them in search of the heavy bunch of keys, but not finding it.

The last drawer of all was stuck and she yanked at it in exasperation, certain that she could hear the clink of keys inside. It came away so suddenly that she lost her balance and sprawled on the floor, the contents of the drawer all around her. With a mutter of triumph, she seized the keys and shinned up the ladder. It only took a moment to replace the book and lock the cabinet again, then she set herself to gather up the things that had fallen from the drawer.

The chief item was a large notebook that had fallen open, spilling out a few sheets of paper. Terri tried to collect them without looking at them, but as she lifted the last one, the words *Elena, my love, my beloved...* seemed to stand out. She averted her eyes, not wanting to read Elena's love letters, even while she wondered what such letters could be doing in Francisco's desk. But she couldn't look away fast enough to avoid seeing the signature at the bottom.

Rufio.

Terri knelt there for a long time, trying to decide what she should do. Many voices shouted in her head, but the one that shouted loudest said that there was something here that threatened Elena, and Elena had the right to know. Slowly she flattened the sheet of paper and read the contents.

Elena, my love, my beloved,
You tell me to forget you, but that's impossible. How can you think for a moment that you could blight my life? To me you are always young. But the truth is that you don't love me.

Every moment is torture without you, thinking of you, dreaming of you, wanting you. I'm sending this to you from the boat. Come away with me and let us live our lives only for each other. If you don't come I shall set sail alone. Without you, my life means nothing to me. Let the sea have it.

Rufio

Terri expelled a long breath. Here was the answer: Rufio's letter threatening suicide, a letter that Elena had never seen, because Francisco had intercepted it.

She piled everything back into the drawer and hurried off, taking the letter with her. She must see Elena without delay. But before she could leave the library, the door opened and Francisco, wearing a black waistcoat and knee breeches, entered and closed it behind him, barring her way.

"I came to look for a book," she said, horribly conscious of the damning letter in her possession.

But he ignored her words. He was holding the pearls. "It wasn't very kind of you to return my gift," he said coldly.

"I wouldn't have accepted them if I'd known how much they were worth."

Francisco's voice had a cutting edge. "And it was even less kind of you to embarrass me by sending them through a servant."

"I'm sorry. I wanted to return them at once and I didn't know where you were—"

"I've been in the house all day, Teresa. How strange that you couldn't find me." His eyes snapped. "I don't think I've ever been treated in such a way by an employee before."

"That's exactly it, Signor Conte," she said firmly. "I'm an employee, and such a valuable gift was not appropriate."

"You didn't adopt these proper airs last night when we went to the Midas. Or were you playing with me to score a point off Maurizio?" He moved a step closer. "I won't allow that, Teresa. It's not—polite."

She drew a deep breath. "Will you please let me pass?"

"Not until you've accepted my pearls again. You will wear them tonight."

"I'm sorry, I can't do that."

"But I insist." He put out a hand to her neck but Terri struck it aside. Francisco's eyes glinted.

"How very proper you are, Teresa. How very suitable such propriety would be—under some circumstances."

"I—will—not—wear—your—pearls," she said emphatically. At that moment, there was a shout from outside the door and a chatter of male voices. "Your guests have arrived, Signor Conte. Let me pass at once or I'll scream for help."

A chilly admiration came into Francisco's reptilian eyes. He stood aside and made no further attempt to touch her as she escaped. She reached the hall in time to see Elena descending the staircase in all her golden glory. A court of gallants had gathered at the bottom and were vying for the honor of taking her arm. She gave a teasing smile that encompassed them all and seemed to be trying to decide between them. Terri hesitated, knowing that she would have to wait until later to show Elena the letter.

Some of the young men noticed her arrival and diverted to her. Elena laughed and winked at Terri, not at all put out by the loss of her cavaliers. She still had four to herself.

"Who's going to escort you in the boat?" one of them asked.

"Nobody," Elena declared. "I'm going to walk. It's not far to St. Mark's Square, and we can all go together." She glanced at Terri, surrounded by spirited young men, and said impishly, "Take the rest of the night off, *cara*. I shall be perfectly all right without you." She allowed one sighing swain to adjust a cape about her shoulders, handed her fan to another and took the arms of the remaining two to make a splendid exit.

There was nothing for Terri to do but follow suit. They made a merry party as they covered the short distance to St. Mark's Square. Terri laughed and flirted from the surface of her mind, but her thoughts were on the letter, safely hidden in her reticule.

The huge piazza was full of colored lights and bizarre costumes. Music filled the air. People danced and sang, and drank and romanced, for it was the last night of Carnival, the last chance to enjoy forbidden pleasures. One of Terri's admirers proposed a drink at Florian's, the old coffeehouse where Casanova himself had once drunk and wooed. She agreed, but the next moment a movement of the crowd gave her the chance she needed. Two eager young men, seeking to put their arms about her waist, found themselves embracing each other, instead. Terri had slipped away and was running as if the Furies were after her.

She raced through the back streets to the Midas, as surefooted now as a Venetian. The first person she saw when she arrived was Bruno. "Where's Maurizio?" she gasped.

"He's gone out with a party of guests. But he left only a short while ago. You might still catch him. He's wearing a *baùtta.*"

"Then how will I know him?" she asked frantically. "There are so many."

"One of the guests is a very fat man in a scarlet Pantalone costume. You'll know *him* without any trouble. That way." He came to the door and pointed. Terri sped away.

Luck was with her. She saw the fat Pantalone after only a few minutes, and there was Maurizio beside him, tall and elegant in the black cloak and white mask. He tensed as he saw Terri and drew apart from his party. "Have you come to torment me some more?" he asked harshly, pulling off his mask.

"Yes," she said. "I've brought you the worst torment of all, Maurizio—the knowledge that you were wrong. Elena isn't responsible for Rufio's death. She never knew he was planning suicide and I can prove it. Here." She pulled him into a brightly lit doorway and thrust the letter into his hands. "He didn't *tell* her he wanted to die. He wrote it to her. I found this letter among Francisco's things. He must have intercepted it. Elena never saw it. Do you understand that? She never knew."

Maurizio leaned again the wall, his shoulders sagging as if he'd received a stunning blow. "It's Rufio's writing," he murmured. "He wrote this to her..."

"But she never received it," Terri repeated. "Francisco had it all this time. You've been avenging yourself on an innocent woman. If anyone is guilty of Rufio's death, it's Francisco."

"Dear God!" he whispered. "What have I done?"

"Unless Leo is found, we may never know what you've done," Terri said bitterly.

He bent his head. "You've every right to punish me with that." A shudder went through him and he pulled himself together. "This isn't the time. There are things to be done first."

"Hey, Maurizio."

The shout came from the scarlet Pantalone who'd turned back to see where his host was. "Wait a moment," Maurizio said, replacing his mask. "I'll talk to them, then we'll—"

His words were cut off by a crowd of brightly dressed revelers that surged against them. For a few moments, there was confusion. Terri was knocked off-balance and fell halfway through the doorway of a little café. She was rescued by a Pulcinella coming out, who caught her and grinned through his mask. "Are you all right?"

"Yes, thank you," she said breathlessly. She looked around for Maurizio but the crowd was thickly packed and pouring along the narrow street like a river in flood. She was knocked sideways again, flung out her hands to steady herself and felt them gripped in another pair of hands. Looking up she was relieved to see the white mask looking down at her. "Thank you," she said again. "Now I want us to go and find Elena."

"Why?"

"Maurizio, how can you ask why? I want her to hear from your own lips that you were wrong, that you know she didn't ignore Rufio's suicide note, because Francisco kept it from her. Surely you can see that she's entitled to that?"

After a moment, he nodded slowly and his grip on her hands tightened. He swung away, drawing her after him. She tried to speak, to tell him they were going the wrong way, but she couldn't shout loud enough above the noise.

At last they reached a small canal where one gondola was waiting. Before Terri could protest, she was hurried down the steps and aboard. The gondola rocked and she clutched Maurizio. "Sit down," he said.

"But I keep trying to tell you—" Even as she spoke, he was pushing her back against the cushions. A snap of his fingers made the gondolier push off and the next moment they were out in the middle of the water. "There was no need for this," she said. "I keep trying to tell you that Elena is in St. Mark's Square. We could have walked it."

"But we're not going to St. Mark's Square."

Something unfamiliar in the timbre of the voice made Terri look up sharply. Before her horrified eyes, the white mask was snatched away to reveal—

"Francisco." The world spun around her. "How did you get here?"

"I've always been here, *cara,*" he said with a cold little smile. "I followed you from the square, hoping to catch you alone. I have important things to discuss with you and I've waited long enough."

"We've nothing to discuss. Let me out of here. I've got to find Maurizio."

"Maurizio can wait, but *I* can't. I've done so much waiting for you, Teresa, and you've played the game very skillfully, I must admit."

"What game? I don't know what you're talking about."

"Oh, I think we can drop the pretense now, don't you? You've been my ideal of a perfect woman since the first moment I saw you, and I'm a man who demands perfection in everything. You know that because you understand me. You've shown it in a thousand ways."

"You're mad. I've done my best to avoid you."

"I know, and I admired you for your discretion. There should be no gossip about my future countess."

"Your—*what?*"

"Elena's day is done. I need a son and I must look elsewhere. You please me, Teresa. Together we'll make fine sons."

Aghast, she tried to push him away but she only made the gondola rock. The gondolier steadied it but seemed otherwise oblivious to what was going on. Terri realized he was Francisco's private boatman who would obey his master, no matter what. She looked wildly around her but they were in a small backwater where the buildings came down directly into the canal. Not a soul was in sight. She tried to cry out but Francisco's hand over her mouth choked off the sound.

"Don't make a sound," he said. "Just listen. It's a pity you found that letter. It's forced my hand rather, but I'd have taken you in the end, anyway."

She twisted her head enough to speak. "You're no better than a murderer. You let Rufio die—"

"Don't be stupid. I didn't want him dead. I wanted him alive and tempting Elena to indiscretions that would help me divorce her. I kept the letter as evidence. I thought that soon there'd be more evidence to back it up. I never dreamed the hysterical boy would really kill himself. When he died, the letter became useless. But now that you've found it, I suppose you'll go blabbing to Elena. So before you do, I'll have to put you in the right frame of mind for our future."

"You're mad," she gasped. "A future with you? I'd rather live in a gutter."

He gave a noiseless laugh that filled her with dread. "My dear! What old-fashioned sentiments. But that was always part of your charm. How ungrateful you are when I'm offering you glory. Those pearls you rejected so disdainfully were just a little down payment." He reached inside his cloak and produced the pearl necklace. "When I honor you with a gift, you do *not* return it," he said through gritted teeth. "Here." He thrust the necklace down the bosom of her dress while she tried to writhe away in disgust. "Now I think it's time you thanked me."

He pressed her back against the cushions. Terri tried to fight him but he had a grip of iron. His face loomed above her in the night, the mouth stretched in a leering grin. "This is always the best part," he said. "The beginning—a new woman whose body offers fresh delights."

His mouth crushed hers with cruel force. She tried to writhe away but his grip was unyielding. Her gorge rose at his kiss and the feel of him trying to drive his tongue between her lips. Her whole body was cold with horror, and fear rose within her as she realized that they were near the palazzo. Once inside, he could do what he liked and no one would help her. The thought of him touching her body, the body that belonged only to Maurizio, lent her strength. She managed to get her mouth free long enough to gasp, "Get away. You disgust me—"

"My dear, what an irresistible invitation. If you'd been willing, you'd have had no charm for me. You've kept me at a distance until I was mad for you—*but no longer.*"

He jerked her back into his arms. Terri fought him madly, dazed at the nightmare that had overtaken her.

She had a strange sensation that the world had slowed down so that she was floating in a dream. Up ahead, she could see a bridge. At one end was the Harlequin figure she'd seen the other night. At the other end stood Elena, staring down at them as though transfixed by what she saw. The gondola glided closer and closer. Terri could feel herself losing the battle. She managed to cry out her despair and the sound echoed through the maze of canals.

Then Elena seemed to come to life, throwing out her arms and screaming, "Francisco, no. *She is my daughter.*"

The words seemed to galvanize Harlequin. In a swift, athletic movement he climbed the rail, stood poised for a moment and leapt down. The gondola rocked as he landed and threw the gondolier into the water. Francisco half rose, his face contorted and vicious, and raised his arm to strike, but then he, too, was in the water, sent flying by a well-aimed punch.

Terri's eyes were fixed on Harlequin's face as he slid down into the seat beside her. Without speaking, he peeled away his mask. *"Leo!"* she cried. "Oh, God, Leo! You're alive." She clung to him, sobbing with joy.

"Of course I'm alive," he said in surprise.

"But I didn't know—you've been missing for four months."

"Four months?" He seemed dazed.

"Where have you been?"

He frowned. "I don't—think I know."

There was a commotion from the bank. Francisco was struggling through the water. A tall figure in a *baùtta* had appeared from the shadows and was there waiting for him. As Francisco reached the bank, the stranger ripped aside his white mask, revealing Maurizio, with murder in his eyes. He grasped Francisco, yanked him ashore and thrust him against the wall.

As the gondola touched the bank, Leo leapt out, with Terri hurrying after him. Francisco was pressing himself flat against the wall, his face full of fear at Maurizio's expression. "You're right to be afraid," Maurizio told him savagely. "It was you who killed my brother."

"You're mad," Francisco said in a choked voice. Maurizio's hands were around his throat.

"Yes," Maurizio agreed. "Mad with the madness of the vendetta."

Terri felt herself paralyzed. She wanted to cry out to Maurizio to stop but something silenced her. She could only watch as the terrible drama was played out to the finale.

Then something happened to Maurizio. He seemed to become aware of her and in the same moment the murder died out of his eyes. "No," he said slowly. "Vendetta is not the way."

"I wouldn't mind a little mild vendetta," Leo observed, oblivious to the seething undercurrents. "I didn't like the way he was treating my sister. How about another sock on the jaw?"

But Maurizio shook his head and put his hand out to restrain Leo. "Scum like that isn't worth the effort," he said. "Leave him to bring his punishment on himself."

His eyes met Terri's, then he turned and his gaze rested on Leo. He closed his eyes and his lips moved in a silent prayer of gratitude.

"Maurizio," Leo said, puzzled, "what the devil—"

"Go," Maurizio told him in a shaking voice. "Go to your sister." He turned away and went to lean on the bridge rail, staring into the water.

Francisco was propping himself up against a wall in a paroxysm of coughing. As he realized he was safe from Maurizio he turned contemptuous eyes on his wife. "Your daughter?" he echoed. "Are you mad?"

Elena faced him proudly. She'd removed her mask and Terri felt they were all seeing this woman for the first time. "Not now, Francisco. I've been mad all these years, but no more." She touched Leo on the shoulder and took Terri's hand in hers. "This is my son and this is my daughter, born when I was a silly child who didn't know what mattered and what didn't. God forgive me, but I gave them away and sold myself to you, but I've paid for that mistake. There hasn't been a moment since then when my heart hasn't broken for the loss of my children. I pray that one day they may find it in their hearts to forgive me."

He hardly seemed to hear her. "Your children," he echoed. "Children. Born before our marriage." His voice rose to a scream. "You've admitted it before witnesses. For this I can annul our marriage and throw you out. You'll have nothing, do you hear? *Nothing.*"

Elena regarded him, flanked by her son and daughter. "You must do as you please. I have all I want."

"Leo, *Leo*, I can't believe it." Laughing and crying, Terri held her brother in a tight embrace. She drew back to look at his face, then hugged him again. He did the same, weeping as freely as she.

He touched the pendant around her neck. "It was that," he said huskily. "When I saw it, I suspected who you were. But I wasn't sure until—'' his eyes met Elena's ''—until our mother acknowledged you.''

They were back in the Palazzo Calvani where Leo had stripped off his wet clothes and donned a towel robe. Terri had gladly discarded her white satin dress for sweater and pants. Perhaps Francisco was also somewhere changing out of his sodden attire, but nobody knew or cared. He'd slunk away quickly.

Elena had hurried her two children home, followed by Maurizio, who seemed content to remain in the shadows. Now Terri realized that they'd been joined by someone else, someone who'd remained hidden until the last minute, then followed them home and slipped in behind them. Terri regarded her, puzzled. "Haven't I seen you somewhere before?" she asked. "Wait—yes, that night—"

"My name is Damiata," the young woman said defiantly. "You came to the apartments."

"I showed my picture of Leo and your neighbor said she'd seen him talking with you. But you denied it."

"I didn't know why you were looking for him. You might have wanted to do harm to my Leo."

The way she said "my Leo" made Terri look at her with new interest. "He was with you all the time, wasn't he?" she said.

"I found him wandering about Venice," Damiata said. "He didn't know who he was or why he was here. I took him home. It was meant to be just for a couple of nights until he felt better. But then I discovered I didn't want him to go."

Leo reached out and took Damiata's hand in his. "She thought I was on the run from the law," he said. "But she never gave me up." He drew her more closely to him. "And now I'll never give *her* up."

He turned back to his sister. "My memory came and went. I knew I had an important reason for being in Venice, but that was all." He looked at Elena who was regarding him with a little smile. "Something drew me here. I felt sure I knew someone who lived in this building, but I couldn't remember who. I hoped that it would come back to me when I was here, but it never did."

"So you kept slipping away," Terri said. "It was you the other night, holding the lion, wasn't it?"

"Yes, it was me. When you looked down at me from the window, I was sure I knew you, but I couldn't remember. I didn't know you were my sister until tonight." He went over to Elena and looked at her.

"You are my son," she whispered. "In my heart I knew it from the first, but I was afraid to speak. But I'm not afraid anymore. My children were lost and are found, and I have nothing more to fear." She burst into sobs and flung her arms around Leo. He hugged her in return, burying his face against her shining hair. Then they both reached out to draw Terri into the circle, and for a moment the three of them stood locked together in total happiness. Damiata watched them, her face forlorn. Maurizio, standing back, also watched, his face unreadable in the shadows.

"When you were born, I held you both in my arms for just a little time," Elena said through her tears. "Then I gave you away—oh, how could I do it?—and my heart broke. I thought the pain of losing you would cease but it never did. Every year I have kept your birthday in tears. But now—now—"

Then Leo held out his hand to Damiata. Instantly, Elena did the same. "Now I shall have two daughters," she said through her tears. "Oh, my children, my children..."

Terri held her mother against her in a wave of happiness such as she'd never thought to know. Here at last was a mother she could love. Her brother, too, was restored to her, and the barrier that had kept her from Maurizio was down at last.

"Maurizio," she said, drawing away from the charmed circle. "Maurizio..."

"He's gone," Damiata said. "He was watching you as if everything else in the world had ceased to exist for him. But when you didn't look up, he went quietly away."

"Oh, no. I must get him back." Terri hurried across the hall and pulled open the big front door. The night was silent but for the faint cries of revelers in the distance. She began to run, calling Maurizio's name as she'd once called Leo's, but there was no reply.

In the distance a *baùtta* fluttered around the corner, but when she chased after him there was nothing to be seen.

The darkness was just beginning to lift as Terri drove a motorboat cautiously across to Murano. At the Midas she'd found Maurizio already gone, nobody knew where. Bruno, strolling home in the small hours with a Columbine on his arm had regarded her gravely and said, "There's a place where I know Maurizio goes when he's troubled. But I've never been there. He never takes anybody to his sanctuary."

"He's taken me," Terri said proudly.

"In that case he's probably waiting for you." Bruno kissed her. "Good luck, *cara*, for his sake more than yours. A nature like yours will always find love, but you're Maurizio's last chance." He wandered away unsteadily, holding on to Columbine as they climbed the stairs.

Now as Terri neared her destination, she was full of fear. Suddenly, it seemed as if the love she'd thought she shared with Maurizio had been only in her imagination. He'd been tortured by guilt about Leo, but now that her brother was all right, Maurizio had discovered that there was nothing else between them. He'd escaped her to avoid embarrassment. Then she would remember Damiata saying, "He was watching you as if everything else in the world had ceased to exist for him."

Which was the truth? She would have no peace until she knew.

As she grew nearer, she could see a light on in the shabby little house of gold, and the next moment Maurizio had come out to catch her line and tie it up. He assisted her onto the bank but released her hand at once and kept his distance.

"I guessed you'd be here," she told him.

"I was afraid you would."

"Afraid? Why are you avoiding me, Maurizio?"

"Isn't it obvious why? We both discovered the truth last night. What else is there to say?"

"I don't know. That's what I came here to find out." She hesitated. Maurizio's silence and uneasiness was making it hard for her. "I had to speak to you because I'm leaving the palazzo today. We both are."

"Both?"

"Elena and I. Francisco's been on the phone to his lawyer but he needn't have bothered. Now she's made her mind up, Elena can't wait to get out. She and Leo are full of plans to go into business together, designing jewelry. She's like a new woman."

They went into Maurizio's kitchen and he started making coffee. "I'm glad it's all ended well for you," he said without looking at her.

"Has it ended well, Maurizio? Tell me."

"You've got Leo back. Your mother has acknowledged you. That was what you wanted. You can be happy now."

"Maurizio, do you know how I knew you'd be here?"

He looked at her. "Because I told you it was my refuge?"

"Partly that. But also because it's February 28th. I read that date on Rufio's tomb. It's exactly one year ago today that he died, isn't it?"

His face softened. "Fancy your remembering such a thing."

"I knew you'd come here to think about him, and I couldn't bear to think of you being alone. The rest of us have got what we want. But you can never have Rufio back."

"How like you to think of that," he said quietly. "You were always generous, more generous than I deserve. Perhaps even generous enough to let me delude myself—but I don't want that kind of delusion."

"Delude yourself about what?" she demanded, her heart beating hard.

"You shouldn't have come here, Teresa. I know the truth. As long as Leo was lost, our need made a kind of emotional dependency for us. We were enemies but no one else understood what we were going through and we could reach out to each other. But now—"

"Now?" she asked, breathless with hope.

"Now I can't hide behind that anymore. I have to look clearly at myself, and what I see I don't like. I see a man who thought he could play God with people's lives, and who ended up nearly killing Leo and destroying you. I see the pride and arrogance that blinded him to everything but himself. I, too, am going away.''

"Where?" The word broke from her in anguish.

"I don't know. A long way away from here, where I can do no more damage."

"The only damage you can do me is to leave me, Maurizio."

"You think that now, but in time you'll see I was right. I poison everything I touch. What can you want with such a man?"

"His love," she cried.

"Even my love is poisoned. Be thankful that you at least managed to escape from me."

"But I haven't escaped. I'll never escape. I belong to you, Maurizio, not because of anything you've done, but because I *choose* to belong to you. I love you. There's no escaping from that, for you or for me."

"You don't know what you're saying," he said roughly. "You don't know what I'm like."

"But I do. I know the worst of you, and the worst is terrible."

"Well then—"

"But the worst of me is terrible, too. I know that now. I too have been eaten up with hatred—"

"You have every right."

"Perhaps. But I've done worse." She moved closer and spoke to him urgently. "Listen to me. After the terrible things I've said to you, you have the right to hear what I'm going to say now." She paused for a moment to look into his eyes. "Like you, I've lashed my hatred to keep it alive. When I felt myself softening toward you, I fought it. I did the very things I blamed you for. You once asked for my understanding and I couldn't give it to you. Isn't it ironic to think I can give it to you now because I know I'm just as bad?''

"That's not true," he said quickly. "It never could be. When I laid hands on Francisco, I wanted to kill him. At one time I think I would have killed him. But last night I couldn't, and it was because of you. My revenge had already created one wasteland, and suddenly I saw that that's all revenge ever creates—waste and desolation. There comes a time when a man has to say that he will accept the pain instead of trying to ease it by hurting someone else, because only in that way can life go on." He took her face between his hands and spoke softly. "Even if I never see you again, my life will go on, because of you."

"Don't talk as though we're going to part," she said passionately. "We can't part now, we've only just found each other."

"Didn't we find each other once before?"

"No, we only thought we did. But it was false because we were both wearing masks. But the masks have gone now, Maurizio, and we can see each other clearly, bad as well as good. I love you. I love *you,* as you are. Only one thing could be worse than what's already happened, and that's if you didn't love me."

"You know better than that. But what right do I have to speak of love to you?"

"The right that I give you. Tell me that you love me. Or better still, show me." When he didn't move, she came close and laid her hand on his cheek. "Show me, Maurizio."

With a groan that came from his very depths, he took her in his arms and covered her lips desperately with his own. "It won't work," he said against her mouth. "I'm a monster—I could never make you happy—"

"You can make me happy now." She led him gently upstairs to the room where they'd once made love, and drew him onto the bed. Although his conscience still lashed him, he had no more strength to resist her will.

Now their lovemaking was different, lacking the frantic sensual urgency of before. There would be time for that in the years ahead, but this time they needed something else: love that was gentle and forgiving, whose tenderness could heal. In the quiet exchange of self for self, they rediscovered each other, and their true selves.

At last Terri rose and opened the shutters. While they'd lain in each other's arms, the sun had come up, making the water glisten and touching the distant domes of Venice with gold. "Once before, we watched the sun rise from this window," she said. "Do you remember?"

He came to stand behind her and rested his head against hers. "That was another man, a sick man—"

"No," she said softly. "Just an unhappy one. But the dawn always returns at last, my darling, and now it's returned for us. Look how golden the sky is. Your mother was right. A house of gold has many rooms. Now it's time for us to start building ours."

* * * * *

Silhouette Books
is proud to present
our best authors, their best books...
and the best in your reading pleasure!

Throughout 1994, look for exciting books
by these top names in contemporary
romance:

DIANA PALMER
Enamored in August

HEATHER GRAHAM POZZESSERE
The Game of Love in August

FERN MICHAELS
Beyond Tomorrow in August

NORA ROBERTS
The Last Honest Woman in September

LINDA LAEL MILLER
Snowflakes on the Sea in September

When it comes to passion,
we wrote the book.

Silhouette®

Silhouette ROMANCE™

First comes marriage.... Will love follow?
Find out this September when Silhouette Romance presents

Join six couples who marry for convenient reasons, and still find happily-ever-afters. Look for these wonderful books by some of your favorite authors:

#1030 *Timely Matrimony* by Kasey Michaels
#1031 *McCullough's Bride* by Anne Peters
#1032 *One of a Kind Marriage* by Cathie Linz
#1033 *Oh, Baby!* by Lauryn Chandler
#1034 *Temporary Groom* by Jayne Addison
#1035 *Wife in Name Only* by Carolyn Zane

Relive the romance... This September,
Harlequin and Silhouette are proud to bring you

by Request™

Marry Me... Again!

Some men are worth marrying *twice*...

Three complete novels by your favorite authors—
in one special collection!

FULLY INVOLVED by Rebecca Winters
FREE FALL by Jasmine Cresswell
MADE IN HEAVEN by Suzanne Simms

If you're looking to rekindle something wild, passionate
and unforgettable—then you're in luck.

Available wherever
Harlequin and Silhouette books are sold.

HARLEQUIN® Silhouette®

HRE0994

Mavericks

If you love MONTANA MAVERICKS, then we've got the calendar for you....

MAVERICK HEARTS

Featuring some of the hottest, sexiest cowboys of the new West!

Plus, purchase a MAVERICK HEARTS calendar and receive FREE, a Country Music Cassette featuring such bestselling recording artists as: Alan Jackson, Clint Black, Brooks & Dunn, and many more! A $10 value!

Lasso yourself a new Western hunk every month!

(limited quantities available)

Look for it this August at your favorite retail outlet, or if you would like to order MAVERICK HEARTS #087 ASTX, send your name, address, zip or postal code along with a check or money order (please do not send cash) in the U.S. for $9.99 plus$1.50 postage and handling for each calendar, and in Canada for $12.99 plus $2.50 postage and handling for each calendar, payable to Maverick Hearts, to:

In the U.S.	In Canada
Silhouette Books	Silhouette Books
3010 Walden Ave.	P. O. Box 636
P. O. Box 9077	Fort Erie, Ontario
Buffalo, NY 14269-9077	L2A 5X3

(New York residents remit applicable sales taxes.
Canadian residents add applicable federal and provincial taxes.) MAVCAL

Only from ▼ *Silhouette*®

where passion lives.